ISBN 978-1-7333595-0-4 Paperbook

ISBN 978-1-7333595-1-1 EBOOK

The characters and events portrayed in this book are fictitious. Any similarity to real persons, living or dead, is coincidental and not intended by the author.

Special Thanks To
Brittany Melton for her editing expertise and professionalism.

DEDICATION

THIS BOOK IS DEDICATED TO ALL MY FRIENDS AND FAMILY THAT HAS CONTRIBUTED TO MY HAPPY EXISTENCE.

Leeanner and Richard Ayers
Melvin and Berlene Ayers
Ludean Williams-Ayers & Evolve Ayers
Mollie Ayers
Monica Ayers
Lolita Ayers
Larry Darnell Ayers
Jacob Ayers
Jerry Ayers
Evolve Ayers Jr.
Malcolm Ayers
Oliver Darrell Ayers
Beverly Ayers
Willie Ayers
Milton and Gloria Ayers
Violet and John Douglas Ayers
Roy and Sheron Ayers
Joe and Christine Ayers
Darthula Cuesta Bass
Antonio and Zenovia Bass
Timothy Bass
Dwight Beasley
Mattie Bee
Mary Clarice and Brady Bolden
Belbert Brasher
Bessie Brasher
Effie Meeks-Brasher and George Brasher
William and Elvira Brasher
Bessie Brasher
Belbert Brasher
Alex Brown
Hope Brown
Rose and Melton Campbell
Verna Campbell
Betty Jean Thomas-Cason
Debora Liles-Clemmons & Bobby Clemmons
Timothy Carlos Cook
Linda Cooper
Rudy Mae Couch
Christine Doss
Gail Ford
Trina Ford
M'Cayla A. Frierson

Johonna and Juan Garrett
Layla Simone Garrett
Lucille and Bobby Garrett
Tyra Lee Hairston
Samuel C. Harris Sr.
Antika Levenia Hancock
Delores and James Harding
Anthony (Tony) Harkley
Lizza and Alfred Henderson
Mary Herod
Estella and Fred Hill
Issah Henderson
Hattie Henderson
Savannah and Henry Henderson
William and Martha Hill
Angela L. Hoard
Malachi Hurt Horner
Murrell Hubbard
Lula Mae Thomas-Hurt
Peggy Hurt
Sean L. Hurt
Doreatha and James Johnson
Evelyn Thomas-Johnson
Dominique Lee Jones
Kaion Lee Jones
Kia L. Jones
Perry Jones
Patricia Jones
Antoinette Lee
Clinton and Lorraine Lee
Sharon Lipscomb
Melba Martin
Pamala Melton
Debbie Milstead
Trena and Jerry Moody
Mary Ollie
Tamara Kalaniuk Palmer
Shirley Patterson
Luberta Perry
Joyce Powell
Claude Lisha Rucker
Clara Bell Sears
Anastacia Shelton
Jessica Shields
Renee Gail Smith
Shonette Sneed
Adrienne Spruill

Eugenia Bass-Steward
Tarneisha Steward
Jessica Liles-Stewart
Barbara Stone
Anthony Henderson-Thomas
Charlene and Anthony Thomas
Anthony (Tony) Thomas Jr.
Barbara Thomas
Brooklyn A J Thomas
Cheticka Thomas-Russell & Robert Russell
Cecil Thomas Sr.
Cecil Thomas Jr.
Cecil Thomas II
Elizabeth and Albert Thomas
Isabella F. Thomas
Izzie Thomas
Jeffrey and Deana Thomas
Jared and Jasmine Thomas
Jerrel Jurial Thomas
Jettson Dane Thomas
Jia Marley Thomas
John Oneal and Pam Thomas
Jonathan Thomas
Justin Jamal Thomas
Kathrine Angelique Thomas
Matthew Thomas
Mattie Henderson-Thomas
Melissa Thomas
Neal Thomas
Roshecka Thomas
Shericka Thomas
Violet Thomas
Virginia Randall and John Henry Thomas
Jennifer Marie Thompson
Jasmine Tweedy
Jessica Thomas-Upshaw
Joseph Keaton Upshaw Jr.
Rochelle and Benny Walker
Carolyn Washington
Cynthia and Harold Washington
Sherry James-Washington
Dion Waters
Anthony Wheeler
Eloise Widgeon
Shirley Young

Chapter 1

The Clearwater family were hurrying through the aisle to find a seat close to the auditorium stage. It was Herman Clearwater's only son's; Calvin's, high school graduation. As the Clearwater family sat down in their seats, Darlene Clearwater, Herman's wife, looked a little misty-eyed. She whispered to her husband, with a dreary look on her face. "Where did the time go? One day I was changing his diapers, and now he is graduating from Burlington High School." "Yes," Herman replied. "He has turned out to be a fine young man." Darlene looked at her husband with a frown on her face and said, "Man, he still has a way to go before I consider him to be a man."

Herman didn't reply; he just looked at his graduation invitation. The graduating class uniquely designed the invitations with their class colors. It was embroidered in green with a shiny gold border written in black calligraphy lettering. He remembered how proud Calvin was when he handed the invitation to him.

Excitement was in the air throughout the auditorium. Herman was thinking about how this was such a significant step in his son's life. Cindy Clearwater, the youngest child of the family and the only daughter, started smiling. She was proud of her brother's achievement and mostly looking forward to him leaving for college. Although they got along well, Cindy could not wait to have the house to herself. "Momma's boy," Cindy said as she listened to her mother discuss her brother. Cindy expected her mother to be more enthusiastic about Calvin graduating. Cindy whispered to her father, "What's up with mom?" "She thinks she is losing a son. You know how close they are. But she will be alright."

The program began, and the audience quieted down. Mr. Grant, the high school principal, was giving his speech to the graduating class when Calvin's Uncle James stood up to go to the restroom. He wanted to hold off but could not help it. Uncle James was trying to proceed to the aisle but began to trip over people's feet. Herman gave him a dirty look because of all the noise that he was making. Mr. Grant glanced up with a confused expression on his face. Herman was so embarrassed, he held his head down and put his hands over his eyes.

The announcer started calling the graduates names just as Uncle James returned to his seat. "Did I miss him?" Uncle James asked Cindy. Before Cindy could answer, Herman replied, "No, just sit down!"

"Calvin Clearwater," the announcer said; the Clearwater family and friends cheered and whistled. Cindy stood up quickly, clapping as Herman tried to pull her back to her seat. Calvin waved and proudly walked off the stage. Darlene clapped, but she wasn't as cheerful as the rest of the family. Herman put his arms around his wife and said, "Don't worry; you have not lost a son."

As the graduation ceremony ended, the Clearwater family found Calvin and greeted him with congratulations. Calvin was talking to some of his friends but stopped to give his mother a big hug. He told his family that he would be going out with his friends for the rest of the day.

"Please don't wait up for me!" Herman smiled and said. "Have a good time, Calvin. Be careful, son." Darlene started to say something, but Herman took her hand and said, "Let's go."

As the Clearwater family walked to the car, Darlene's eyes filled up with tears. Cindy began to laugh. "I am counting down to the day when I can take over Calvin's room. His room is bigger than my room and has a larger closet. We should just get rid of all his stuff and make my old room into a walk-in closet."

"What?" Darlene asked as she turned and looked at Cindy. Cindy continued to laugh and said," I was just joking, mom." "You better be kidding! We will never get rid of his belongings. He will always have a place in our home."

The family was in the car, discussing where they would like to eat while fastening their seatbelts. Darlene seemed to be in a daydream as she slowly fastened her seatbelt. Herman asked, “Darlene, where would you like to go to for dinner?” Darlene did not answer. You could tell her mind was somewhere else. Herman said, “Darlene!” Darlene looked at Herman and replied, “YES!” Herman impatiently asked, “What are you thinking about?” Darlene finished fastening her seat belt, looked at her husband, and said, “Oh nothing, I was just wondering where the time went.” Herman ignored Darlene’s response because he did not want to feed into her sad mood. He thought for a minute and said, “Restaurants will be full because of the school graduations. Let’s just eat what we have at home.” “Sounds good to me,” Cindy remarked. Uncle James said, "Drop me off at home. I will eat there" "OK," said Herman and proceeded to drive out of the parking lot.

The moon was rising as the night started turning dark. It was late in May; the temperature was seasonably cooler than most years. Herman had opened the window when he arrived home from the graduation to let some fresh air into the house.

He got out of his chair to close the window. Although it was still early, Herman decided to clear his things from the living room and get ready to call it a night. The graduation ceremony took a toll on him and he was ready to retire to bed. Darlene was still watching television when Herman said to her, "goodnight."

"You going to bed early tonight Herman?" Herman replied with an exhausted, "I woke up too early this morning and thought my body could use more rest." Darlene started stretching out on the couch and said, "I will just wait for Calvin." Herman was almost at the top of the stairs when Darlene finished her sentence. He turned around and said, "Darlene, you can't shelter the boy his entire life. Allow Calvin to have some fun. It is time for you to stop treating him like a child. He is a responsible person, and we need to be more flexible. Just relax and come to bed early with me. We can watch a movie. I will give you one of my intense back massages. You seem to need it." Darlene wanted to say something but changed her mind. She stood up and walked toward the stairs. Herman waited until Darlene started walking up the stairs. He reached for his wife's hand, and they went upstairs together.

Before entering their bedroom, Herman opened the door to Cindy's room to check on her. She was on the laptop with earphones in her ears. "We are going to bed now," he announced, but Cindy did not turn around. Herman just shut the door and went into his bedroom.

Darlene was sitting on the bed. She thought about how she wanted to wait until Calvin came home. It was Herman's unusual facial expression that convinced her to give in. She felt it was not worth arguing. Although Herman was a loving husband, he could get his point across. So,

Darlene decided just to let it go. "Now, relax," Herman said as he proceeded to massage her shoulders. That seemed to calm Darlene down, and before you know it, they both had fallen asleep.

Chapter 2

Calvin rushed to turn off the alarm as he entered the house. It was so loud. He put his finger in his left ear as his right hand quickly punched the numbers. The noise subsided; Calvin looked around to see if anyone had woke up. He waited at the bottom of the stairs for a couple of minutes, wondering if someone would come out of their room. There was no movement, so Calvin went into the living room to relax on the couch. He was finally able to enjoy a peaceful moment after all of the chaos from the graduation day.

Calvin sat on the couch, pulled out his phone, and texted his friend Jerry to tell him that he made it home. Jerry was his best friend and in the same graduating class. They had known each other since elementary school, but their personalities were very different. Jerry enjoyed playing football. He was the quarterback for Burlington High School. Calvin did not participate in any sports. He enjoyed studying geology and had a hobby of rock collecting.

When Calvin was a sophomore in high school, the Clearwater family vacationed in Hawaii. It was during the volcano tour Calvin became interested in geology. He was fascinated with the earth's formation. He began collecting rocks and started participating in activities associated with the high school's geological society. In his senior year, Calvin won an award for writing a paper on how coal mining has affected the earth. This award was a significant component that influenced him to pursue a career in geology. Although he liked science, he never considered pursuing a career in the field. Once he won the geological award, it helped boost his confidence to work in this area of science.

Jerry texted Calvin back; his message indicated that he was still hanging out with his friends. Jerry seemed to be surprised that Calvin was home. He didn't notice Calvin had left until he received the text message. Jerry was too busy having fun at the restaurant, eating, and watching sports on the television. His celebration group consisted of his football teammates. Jerry and Calvin did not run in the same circle, but Jerry decided to invite Calvin to join them to celebrate graduating anyway. Calvin accepted because he did not have another invitation.

It was early during the celebration that Calvin started to feel out of place. The conversations and inside jokes did not make Calvin feel like a part of the group. As time went on, he felt more and more uncomfortable, and when he thought no one was looking, he left. Jerry urged Calvin to join them at one of their classmate's party later on that night. They planned to meet up with some female acquaintances from school, but Calvin declined. He texted that he had a headache and was calling it a night. As Calvin started to go upstairs to his bedroom, he received a text from one of his geological society friends.

Some of the members had decided to meet at a local restaurant called Tommy's to celebrate graduation. It was a spur-of-the- moment decision, and they were texting everyone to see if they could meet at the restaurant. Calvin instantly became rejuvenated. He immediately replied "yes" and headed out the door, forgetting to put on the alarm.

The next morning before Darlene walked downstairs, she opened the door and peeked into Calvin's room. He was sound asleep, snoring profusely. Darlene smiled as she quietly closed the door. Herman was already at the table drinking coffee when Darlene entered the kitchen. "I see Calvin made it home," she said. "Yes, all safe and sound. I told you that there was nothing to worry about, honey." Cindy came running down the stairs with her drum sticks in hand. "Who is going to take me to band practice?" It was Saturday, and she had practice every Saturday at 11:00 a.m. on the school field. Usually, Calvin would have taken her to practice, but since he was still asleep, Darlene volunteered. Give me ten minutes to get ready. "Well, hurry, mom, I don't want to be late. It is our last practice before school is out for the summer." Darlene glanced at her and said, "It will not take me long!" Within fifteen minutes, they were heading to the car.

At noon Calvin came downstairs. Darlene and Cindy had not returned home from band practice. In the study, Herman was reading the news on his laptop when he saw Calvin pass by the door. "Good afternoon," Herman said with a smile. "Did you have fun?" Calvin hesitated and said, "Yea, I guess so," with an exhausted look on his face.

"I met up with some of my friends in the geological society last night. We discussed a geological project this summer sponsored by the University of Michigan. The University is looking for high school graduates to search Michigan's Upper Peninsula for unique rocks that contain the mineral sodalite. I would like to join them on this expedition, which is strictly on a volunteer basis. We must pay for our expenses."

Herman was still reading the news on his laptop, listening to Calvin. He became engrossed with the local headlines. However, when he heard him say, volunteer, he stopped and turned around to look at Calvin. "I think this project will be a great experience for your career, son, but we can't afford for you to volunteer your services. Since you will be attending college this fall, you need to work to assist us with some of your educational expenses." 'Alright.' Calvin said as he lowered his head in disappointment. Herman turned around to continue to read the news; he said, "Don't worry, I have got you a job at my friend's pizza restaurant. I confirmed this with him yesterday. He has agreed to allow you to deliver pizza." "Great, this is going to be a fun summer!" Calvin whispered to himself as he walked away.

Chapter 3

It was the end of summer; Herman and Cindy was seated at the table on the patio for dinner in the backyard. There was no shade to protect them from the beaming hot sun. Occasionally a gentle cool breeze would blow on their faces while they wait for dinner. So far, summer had been uneventful for the Clearwater family. For the first time in weeks, their schedule allowed them to eat a family meal together. Herman took advantage of this situation to grill some of his infamous chicken. His grilled chicken was a family favorite.

He took so much pride in grilling that he had made unique sauces for the various meats he cooked. The sauce made for his grilled chicken was by far the tastiest. Darlene carried the remaining food to the table as she looked around to make sure everyone was there. "Where is Calvin?" Darlene asked, sitting down in her chair. "I thought this was his day off?" Calvin came through the door, "I went to the store for some bottled water. I am hungry and ready to eat!" Darlene smiled and said, "We have one of your favorites, dad's famous grilled chicken."

As they ate their dinner, Cindy looked down at the calendar on her phone and said, "I know how many days are left until Calvin finally leaves for college." Calvin replied, "How many?" "Well, said Cindy, approximately," and before she could finish her sentence, Darlene ordered her to put her phone down and eat. Cindy was aware of the family's rule of no phones allowed at the dinner table. Darlene looked at Cindy, saying, "you know the rules, young lady!" Cindy slowly put down her phone and proceeded to say, "Approximately 45 days." Calvin responded, "YES! That's what I figured. I can't wait."

Calvin made that statement because his summer had been boring. All he did was work almost every day at the pizza restaurant. He settled into a routine of going to work, coming home, and going straight to bed. Calvin stayed focused on saving his money to buy extra school supplies. That meant working through the weekends and most nights during the weekday delivering pizzas.

He made friends with his coworkers and some customers at the restaurant but hoped he could enjoy some summer activities with his geological friends. Calvin realized that he had a short period to earn the money he needed for school. So Calvin buckled down and continued to work hard and save his money. He would periodically take the time to talk to his friends on the telephone. Sometimes they stopped by the pizza restaurant to visit. A couple of weeks ago, some of his friends visited him at the restaurant. He sat with them between pizza deliveries. His friends ate pizza and discussed what was happening. One of his friends named Joe began to discuss Sarah Madison. Calvin had a crush on Sarah for a couple of years. He was surprised to hear Joe mention her name. Calvin sat back and relaxed, ready to listen to the gossip about Sarah, but suddenly, he was requested to deliver a pizza. "Save that conversation until I come back because I want to hear this." Joe said, "OK, I will wait."

Calvin left to deliver the pizza to a customer in a nearby neighborhood. He rushed back, almost running a stop sign. As he entered the restaurant, his friends were still in the booth eating pizza. Once Calvin sat down, he said, "Joe, what were you saying about Sarah?" Joe looked up and said, "oh yeah, she is engaged to Jerry." "You know Jerry?" Joe continued, "Jerry, the quarterback from high school, your buddy." Calvin looked puzzled and said, "I didn't know they were dating." Someone said, "I think they have been dating for about a year and a half but didn't want anyone to know." Calvin's voice became softer as he repeated, "a year and a half!" Joe said, "Now everyone knows because she is showing off her ring." Calvin appeared to be a bit down as he walked toward the kitchen to pick up the next pizza order. Joe noticed Calvin's mood had changed. Very puzzled, Joe said, "Dude, what is wrong with you? You look so sad. Don't worry, we will come back to visit you soon and give you more updates." Joe thought that Calvin was upset because they were leaving, but that was not the problem. Calvin was broken hearted. No one knew he had a crush on Sarah, and he would never admit it to anyone. "Let us say our goodbyes now because we will not be here when you come back from your delivery," said Joe. Calvin waved goodbye as he walked to the kitchen to pick up the pizza for delivery.

The sun was setting while the Clearwater family was enjoying their dessert. Cindy said, "Calvin, why didn't you tell me about Jerry's engagement?" "Tell you?" Calvin replied, "I just learned this a couple of days ago from some of my friends." You mean Jerry did not say anything?" Cindy responded. Calvin looked a little uncomfortable and said, "No, I heard it was a secret." "A secret well, I saw Sarah, and she showed me her ring, it's not a secret anymore." "I guess not," Calvin commented while shrugging his shoulders.

Herman noticed Calvin's mood had changed as they discussed Jerry's engagement. Herman interjected, "you would think that if Jerry was such a good friend, he should have told you about his engagement himself. How inconsiderate of him not to tell you, and you had to hear it from other people. Don't worry, son, soon you will be off to college, and you're going to forget about all of this." Herman was hoping talking about going to college would cheer Calvin up. "Sure, dad, soon this will all be in the past."

They were clearing the table when Darlene started talking about Calvin preparing for college. Herman said he didn't think it was a good idea for Calvin to have a car during his first year. “Dad, Come on, Please!" Calvin said with a sad demeanor, "You said that this was my car!" "It is, but I need to see how this first year of college works out before I let you take the vehicle on campus." Calvin knew it was no use in discussing it any further. So he started walking from the table, feeling very disappointed.

Darlene said, "Everyone stop. I have an announcement to make. Your father and I have a surprise." Cindy and Calvin stopped and looked at each other. “We have decided to take a short vacation to your Aunt Barbara’s house.” “Aunt Barbara's house," Cindy said. Herman replied, "Yes, since we have not had a vacation this year, your Aunt Barbara thought it would be nice for us to visit for a fun weekend." “What about work?” Calvin asked. Herman replied, "I have cleared the time off with your boss at the restaurant.” Cindy and Calvin paused and looked at each other and said sarcastically, "Great!”

Chapter 4

The weekend at Aunt Barbara's was not that enjoyable to Calvin and Cindy. The only fun they had was when Herman and Darlene dropped them off at the mall. Cindy did some shopping with the money she had saved, and Calvin went to the arcade to keep himself occupied.

Aunt Barbara was a nice person but acted a little strange. She did not have an internet connection in her home and still used a record player to play her old school music. The music was always blasting whenever she cooked. Aunt Barbara enjoyed cooking while singing to her favorite songs.

On the ride back from Aunt Barbara's, Herman was very talkative. He got overly excited to have visited his only sister. Darlene was driving and just listening to Herman reminisce about his childhood. Herman kept mentioning how Barbara reminded him of his mother. He turned around, looked at Calvin and Cindy, sitting in the back seat, and asked, "Did you guys have fun?" Calvin and Cindy looked at each other and said, "Yes, we did," giving each other a nudge. They did not want to hurt their father's feelings.

Cindy and Calvin were glad to be going home where things would return to normal. However, that was not exactly what was awaiting the Clearwater family because the next day, they had to prepare to take Calvin to college.

The following day was pure chaos around the Clearwater household because they waited until the last minute to pack Calvin up for college. The summer was over. On Monday morning, the family was driving Calvin to the university. Since he was attending a university in North Carolina, they wanted to make sure that he didn't forget anything because it was too far to come back.

Cindy was yelling from her room to Calvin to see if he wanted to take her small alarm clock. Darlene was trying to find the gift cards Calvin received for graduation. Herman was downstairs signing the consent forms Calvin needed to stay at the dormitory. Meanwhile, Calvin was in his room, packing his suitcase, feeling a little nervous about leaving home. Calvin couldn't allow his friends or family to know that he was afraid of being on his own. Everyone was so proud of him, he didn't want to let them down.

Calvin looked around the room, contemplating what to pack; his eyes became fixed on a rock that he found on the class trip which Sarah attended. At that point, he had to sit down on the bed and started looking at her photo on his phone. His mind wondered why he never heard from Jerry or Sarah the entire summer. Now he is going to college and probably won't ever see them again. Calvin could not help but still feel heartbroken. As Darlene entered his room waving the gift cards, he snapped right out of his sentimental mood and smiled.

"I knew you had my cards, he said to his mother. "I didn't realize that I had them. I guess I had put them in the drawer in my room. Do you want them, or should I hold on to them?" Darlene asked. "I will take them." "Are you sure because I can keep the cards until you unpack at the dormitory," Calvin looked at his mother with a smile and said, "Ma, I can keep up with all of my belongings. I am not a baby." "I'm sure you can. After all, next week, you will be on your own!" "Wonderful," Calvin said as his mother gave him the gift cards. She halfway smiled and said, "I can't believe you are all grown up." Darlene lowered her head and left the room.

Calvin continued to pack while thinking about the Jerry and Sarah situation. Little did anyone know Calvin was taking the engagement very hard. Every night before bed, he would stare at Sarah's picture. It was a selfie picture taken of him and Sarah when they were on a class trip. The class trip was two years ago, and that is when he kissed her. He was excited to ask her out after the trip. But Sarah started distancing herself, and he didn't feel comfortable asking her out. Calvin couldn't forget the memories, and Sarah stayed on his mind. He was not only heartbroken over Sarah but disappointed that his best friend, Jerry, never let him know what was going on between the two of them.

As his anxiety was getting the best of him, Herman entered the room. He gave Calvin the signed documents and noticed the troubled look on his face. "What's wrong, son?" "Nothing, dad."

Herman knew something was bothering him, but Calvin didn't want to tell him. Herman attempted to make Calvin feel better, so he proceeded to joke around about him leaving home. "Just think, no more of your mother checking on your every move or driving Cindy around town. You will be free as a bird." Herman began to laugh, but Calvin didn't say anything. He just continued to pack.

Herman wasn't comfortable leaving Calvin's room with him feeling depressed. He had to think of something that would snap Calvin out of his sad mood. "Son, this should be the most exciting time in your life." Calvin never looked up. He just continued to pack and said, “I am excited but feel just a little anxious.” “Don’t let your anxiety get the best of you.” Calvin still did not respond. At this point, Herman thought about the technique the therapist taught Calvin for anxiety.

When Calvin was sixteen, Herman sent him to see a therapist because he exhibited abnormal anxious behavior before taking school tests. He only attended a couple of sessions and refused to participate anymore. Herman didn't insist that he attend any more sessions because it seemed like he didn't need to go. Since then, Herman never noticed evidence of Calvin being anxious up until now.

"Calvin remember the technique the therapist taught you?" Herman said. "Wait a minute!" Herman left the room and returned with a small zipped up bag. "Put whatever is making you anxious into this bag." Calvin took the bag from Herman's hand. He remembered the exercise that the therapist practiced with him for his anxiety. "Are they all in the bag?" Herman asked, "Now, zip it up and hand it to me." As Calvin handed Herman the bag, Herman looked down at his phone and said, the plane is leaving in the next hour, destination, Never to Land, and I want this bag to be on it." Calvin began to laugh. "Your right, dad, I want this bag on a plane never to land again! Just stay high up in the clouds." Calvin said as he handed the bag to his father, and they started to laugh. "Now, Calvin, you can have a fresh start in college without any worries." "Get a good night's sleep son, and I will take care of this bag." Calvin began to feel relieved. He finished packing and laid down to sleep. He started dozing off. As his eyes closed he kept saying to himself, "stay in the clouds, never to land."

The next morning started with an air of confusion throughout the Clearwater household. Everyone was rushing around doing last-minute packing. Herman was the only one who remained calm. The family came downstairs one by one looking exhausted. Herman had already made breakfast and was acting a little pleased with himself. "So, I guess everyone is ready?" He asked. "I finished packing last night. I am not sure why everyone is still running around." No one was paying attention to Herman; they were eating their breakfast, not talking. Then finally, Darlene said, "I guess we are ready to go after we eat. Has everyone put their bags by the door so we can load them in the car?" Everyone nodded their head. Herman commented, "Why isn't anyone acting excited? Just relax, and we will be on our way soon. Calvin and I will load the car." Cindy said, "I don't know why I need to come on this trip. I can stay home and practice on my drums!" Darlene said, "This is a family affair, and it will be about six months before we will see your brother again. I am sure you want to see where he will be living." "Not really,'" Cindy replied as she left the table.

The loaded car was running, and everyone was getting settled in their seats. Herman decided to be the first one to drive. The trip would take over ten hours, and they planned to go straight through. Darlene will take over driving after five hours. Everyone got comfortable in their seat. Darlene pulled the headrest back and closed her eyes. Cindy put her earphones in her ears to listen to some music. Calvin was looking out the window. He knew it would be a while before he would see his neighborhood again. As the car drove out of the community, Calvin looked back and saw the beautiful clouds. He remembered the conversation he had with his father the night before. A smile suddenly came to his face as he continued to look at the sky while silently saying, "Never to land."

Chapter 5

People were walking everywhere at the crowded campus as the Clearwater family drove toward the dormitory. They arrived in front of the dormitory building but did not know where to park. Darlene was in the driver's seat, so Herman went inside the building to get directions. Herman walked through the front door; Darlene turned her head toward the back seat to talk to Cindy and Calvin. "I can't believe we will not see you again until Thanksgiving." Cindy chimed in, "that is less than six months away. I am sure he will survive until then!" Calvin and Cindy laughed as Darlene turned around with a frown on her face. Herman returned and gave Darlene directions on where to park.

Calvin's dorm room was located on the second floor. They entered the building with the first load of boxes and waited on the elevator. The elevator took ten minutes to arrive. The elevator finally came, already full of people. It was move-in day at the dorm, seems like everyone was moving in at the same time. After two more tries to get on the elevator, they gave up and used the stairs. The family was exhausted as they put the last box into Calvin's room. They rested awhile, then Cindy and Herman went out to find something to eat. Darlene and Calvin began unpacking and decorating the room. Calvin's roommate had not arrived, so Calvin picked the side of the dorm room he wanted. Darlene started taking over arranging his area, but Calvin had to stop her. He insisted that she step back and allow him to set up the room his way. It was hard for Darlene to relinquish control. But she stepped back and followed Calvin's lead on decorating his room. The room was small, so it did not take a long time to arrange everything.

Cindy and Herman returned with sandwiches. The family laughed and talked about old times as they ate. After they had finished, Herman said, "Let's get ready to go. It's getting late, and we must register at the hotel. Darlene commented, "Give me a few more minutes." Cindy and Herman glanced at one another; Herman said, "Honey, it's time to cut the apron strings." "Yes, mom!" Calvin agreed, "I will be fine." Darlene said, "OK, we will be back tomorrow morning." Herman replied, "No, we will not; we will be driving home right after breakfast. We will call you before we leave to make sure you do not need anything." "OK," said Calvin as he produced a fake smile on his face. He did not want his family to know that he was growing nervous by the minute. The thought of them leaving and him being on his own was a concern. However, he put on a happy face, walked his family to their car, hugged everyone, and waved goodbye. When they left, Calvin went back to his room and watched the freshman orientation online. In the middle of the presentation, he fell asleep. He woke up around three in the morning and changed into his pajamas, then laid down to go back to sleep.

The next morning Calvin woke up, looked around and was a little confused. For a brief moment, he had forgotten he was not at home but in the dormitory. As Calvin slowly sat up in bed, it came to him that he was on his own at school. The thought of being there without his family made him a little anxious. The room was empty and quiet. He could hear people walking around in the hallway. His roommate wasn't supposed to arrive until later in the afternoon. Instead of sitting around in the room by himself, Calvin decided to explore the campus. He showered, put on his clothes, and left.

Calvin took time, scrolling through the grounds of the campus. He was carefree because he had registered for all of his classes and had nothing to do all day. It was a sunny day, perfect weather for walking. There were so many people with different styles and ethnicities. This type of environment was very diverse compared to his hometown. The campus landscape was beautiful. He sat down on a bench by a waterfall to admire the landscape and people watch. Calvin sat for about an hour before he became hungry and decided to go to the food court. The food court was located in the Student Union Building.

He entered the Student Union Building, instantly feeling overwhelmed because there were so many people. Calvin went straight to the food court and purchased a slice of pizza and salad. He did not feel comfortable enough to sit at a table to eat. With his food in hand, Calvin quickly left out the building. He headed back to the dorm to eat his lunch. Strolling across the campus, he heard someone call his name.

"Calvin, Calvin Clearwater," he stopped and turned around. He looked but did not recognize anyone, so he turned back around and started to walk again. Before he could take a step, someone tapped him on his shoulder. "I thought that was you," the voice said. Calvin could not believe his eyes; it was Susan Walker. Susan use to live next door to him until her family moved from the neighborhood a few years ago. She was smiling and gave him a big hug. "It has been a long time," she said. Calvin replied, "What a small world. I didn't know you went to school here."

"Yes. It is my second year here. I like it here, but it took me a while to adjust to this large campus. Sometimes it feels a little awkward because the campus is so big." "I completely understand. It is my first day here, and already I feel like a fish out of water." Susan smiled, took his hand, and said, "I am adjusted to it now. Don't worry. I will show you around." They went back into the Student Union, where Susan purchased her lunch. Calvin and Susan left the building and went under a shady tree to eat.

Susan was a grade ahead of Calvin. She moved during her sophomore semester in high school. They initially called each other the first year after she left, but the calls tapered off. As they ate and talked, their friendship started to rekindle. Calvin said, "I am so glad we ran into each other. Now I know someone around here." Both of them smiled and began laughing. Calvin explained how his parents had just left going back home, and he finished registering for all of his classes. Susan asked, "Did you get all the classes you wanted?" "Yes, indeed. I am so excited about taking this first year's science course because it is my best subject!" He told Susan about the science award he won in his senior year. Susan became excited, opening her eyes a little wider as she snapped her fingers. "Science class, I have an idea. I put off taking this course because science is a hard subject for me. But I need this course as part of my curriculum. Let's take this science class together! With your help, I am sure I can pass it. What do you think?" Calvin seemed thrilled, "I think it will be fun taking this course together. Let's go so you can register before the class is full." Susan explained that she needed approval from the Financial Office first before adding another class to her schedule. She quickly took Calvin's hand and proceeded to walk fast toward the Financial Office.

Susan was pointing out the different buildings as they walked. "You will learn your way," she said, moving swiftly around students.

They were walking so fast Calvin knew he would not remember the building. He had a map of the campus in his pocket. Calvin didn't mention it. He just kept up with the pace. Every so often, he noticed Susan would speak to people she recognized as they hurried along. She was not a popular girl on campus because she did not participate in any college activities. However, Susan knew people on campus from the previous year. It occurred to Calvin he hadn't seen anyone he knew that whole day except for Susan.

The Administrative Building was crowded with people walking everywhere. The Financial Office was located on the third floor. Walking through the hall to the Financial Office made Calvin feel a little nervous because of the crowd. He grasped Susan's hand tighter. When Susan felt him tighten his grip on her hand, she looked at him with a smile saying, "don't worry, I got you." Calvin felt more relaxed as they continued to walk toward the office.

Susan took a number when they entered the lobby of the office. They sat down in the arranged chairs and waited for her number to be called. It was not long before Susan's number was called, then she went to the back room to speak with an advisor. Calvin noticed how the area was filling up as he patiently waited for Susan to return. About the time Susan returned from the back, there was standing room only in the lobby. She stood still and looked for Calvin. Her eyes wandered around the room. She became fixated on a couple standing in the corner. Calvin stood up and motioned for Susan. The waving of Calvin's hand broke her stare. Calvin and Susan began to walk out the door. Susan passed by the couple in which she had noticed. They spoke to her. Keeping her head forward, she never looked at them. She simply waved her hand, saying hello, and kept moving. Walking through the hall, Calvin realized Susan's demeanor had changed. All day, Susan was happy and upbeat. Now her mood was different "Did you get your approval?" Calvin asked. "Oh, yes," she said. Calvin felt a little puzzled, wondering what could have brought on this change in her. Calvin asked, "You seem a little down. What is going on?" "I will tell you when we get out of here," Susan whispered."

They made their way out the doors of the building, walking at a slower pace than before. "Can you tell me now?" Susan replied in a soft, sad voice, "Did you see the couple I waved to in the office lobby? That guy is my ex-boyfriend". "Oh, yea." "Yes, I see he quickly moved on dating again." "How do you know that's his girlfriend?" "People told me about them. Now I see it for myself."

Susan's pace became slower and slower as they walked across the campus grounds. "Since you have approval, now you should go to your dorm and register online for the class before it fills up. Susan, you can't lose your momentum now." "I know you are right, but I was a little startled to see him standing there with her." Calvin felt terrible for Susan. He didn't want to leave her in such a depressed mood. "Shake it off, Susan, and move on." "OK, I will try," Calvin noticed that telling her to shake it off did not uplift her spirits.

He thought of something else to do. Let's go for ice cream; the treat is on me. You can take the ice cream back to your room and eat it while registering." "No, thank you, Calvin. I will go to the dorm and register."

Calvin still did not feel comfortable, leaving Susan feeling disappointed. He cared about Susan and wanted her to be happy. So he thought of one more thing to do before they departed. "Tell you what," Calvin said, "I will teach you a technique I learned that might help you put this ex-boyfriend situation behind you." "Technique?" Susan said as they stopped and sat on a bench. Calvin put both of Susan's hands in his, “Close your eyes and imagine you are packing this heartbreak into a suitcase," he stated. Susan felt reluctant but closed her eyes anyway. "OK, my eyes are closed." She was just amusing Calvin because she saw he was trying very hard to cheer her up. "Now put that problem in a suitcase and close it." Susan began to chuckle. "Open your eyes and hand me the suitcase." Susan motioned, handing the suitcase to Calvin. "Where are you going to take this suitcase?" Susan asked with a smile. "I am putting it on the next flight, destination Never to Land. I am sending this suitcase that contains your broken heart above the clouds. You don't have to worry about it anymore because it will never land." Susan thought that it was sweet of Calvin to try to cheer her up. "Are you feeling better now?" Calvin asked. Susan did not want to disappoint him, so she said, "I think this technique did the trick." Susan began to smile, "that is so clever. I feel better already." They both stood up and headed to their dorm. Calvin was feeling proud of himself because he thought he had helped his friend. "This is my telephone number in case you don't have it. Give me a call when you register for the class. My roommate should be in the dormitory by now. I am going to check him out." They hugged each other and walked away. As they took a few steps, Susan turned back and yelled to Calvin, "Don't forget to put that suitcase on the flight, Never to Land!" Calvin turned around with a smile and said I wouldn't!"

Calvin arrived at his dormitory room to find his roommate Alex Martin putting down his boxes. They introduced themselves and shook hands. Alex had just arrived and was trying to unload his car. Calvin learned that he drove to campus by himself from the Midwest. He thought how brave of Alex to drive this far all by himself. Calvin helped Alex carry his boxes to the room. After unloading the car, the two proceeded to the Student Union so Alex could get something to eat. They sat in the Student Union chatting, getting to know each other. It was Alex's first year also, and he didn't seem to know anyone on campus either. Calvin said to Alex, "I have been walking around campus all day, and I know only one person." Alex said, "I don't know anyone here. That is the reason I chose this university. I wanted to get as far away from family and friends as possible. A fresh start is what I wanted because I was tired of the boring town where I lived." He said with a smile. Calvin looked around and said, "I guess we will get to know some people as the year goes on." "I guess so," said

Alex. They finished their meal and went back to the dormitory.

Chapter 6

It was a month since Calvin arrived on campus. He learned his way around the university and had been feeling more confident. Calvin seemed to be adjusting to campus life. The only problem he had was waking up on time to attend his morning class. His first class started at 9:00 a.m. Both he and Alex had similar schedules, yet they were struggling every morning when it came time to wake up.

During the first week of classes, Calvin asked his mother to help wake him up by calling each morning. The alarm clock they used did not seem to do the trick. When he lived at home, he never had to wake up in the morning on his own. Every morning his mother would open the door to his room and called his name until he sat up in bed. So waking up on his own was an adjustment for him.

His mother was more than happy to assist her son. Faithfully she would call Calvin and just let the phone ring until he answered it.

Everything worked out well until his father learned of the arrangement. Herman immediately put a stop to it. He insisted his wife let Calvin stand on his own two feet and wake himself. Darlene knew Herman was right, but she did not want to disappoint Calvin. It was difficult for her to tell him the morning calls had to stop. As Darlene told Calvin about ending the wake-up calls, Calvin realized his father was behind putting a stop to it. He noticed by the tone of his mother's voice she didn't want to stop. Calvin knew Darlene felt terrible, so he told her he could work it out, not to worry. When she hung up the telephone, she felt a little sad. Now Calvin and his roommate had no choice but to wake up to the alarm on their own. They developed a strategy to wake up on time. Two separate alarms would be set to go off within minutes of each other. It seemed to work out fine. Not only did they wake up in time for class, but they had time to get some breakfast.

All of Calvin's classes were in large classrooms. Each class he attended was full of students. Calvin did not try to make friends with any of the students in his classes. He would just go in, sit in the back, and leave after the lecture. The science class was different. In that class, Susan and Calvin would always sit together. Susan knew a couple of people in the class and introduced them to Calvin.

He didn't bother to make friends with anyone. Calvin mostly stayed to himself. Occasionally he would eat at the food court located in the Student Union Building with Alex or Susan. Mainly he would eat in his room. Every night before dinner, Calvin would call home. He enjoyed talking to his family and keeping up with what was happening at home. Calvin felt a little homesick so talking to his family cheered him up. He kept those feelings to himself and only expressed how happy he was living on campus to them.

One day while Calvin was studying in his dorm, Alex rushed in full with excitement. "I want to attend this convention," Alex said, smiling. He was holding a flyer about a convention given by two paranormal television celebrities. Calvin read the flyer and was surprised that Alex wanted to attend the convention. "I didn't know you believe in the paranormal." "I sure do. I saw a ghost once, and that made me a believer." "A ghost, are you sure?" Calvin asked with a frown on his face. "When I was fourteen, my friends took me on a ghost hunt, and we saw a ghost. After seeing that ghost, I started researching the paranormal and found it to be fascinating". Alex proceeded to show Calvin books he had bought about the paranormal. Calvin rolled his eyes at Alex, "Ghosts, I don't believe in that stuff. I believe in science, and, according to science, ghosts do not exist." "Don't have such a closed mind. I want you to attend the convention with me. We can go out to dinner before attending the convention. It will be good to get away from campus." "But I am a skeptic." "You don't have to believe in the paranormal to attend the convention." "Can you find someone else to attend?" Calvin asked. "No, not really, I don't know anyone on campus that I feel comfortable asking except you, and I do not want to go alone,"

Calvin saw how excited Alex was about the convention and did not want him to go by himself. So Calvin agreed to go. Alex wanted to continue talking about the paranormal, but Calvin stopped his friend. He told Alex that he had to study for an upcoming test and will discuss the supernatural later. Alex said, "Don't forget to mark the date on your calendar. It will be a special night, and I can't wait." Calvin reluctantly marked his calendar, and continued to study.

Calvin was making good grades in his science class. He had received high scores on two science tests. Susan barely passed both of the tests. Calvin was concerned that Susan's scores were very low on both tests and offered to help her study. Susan thought it was a great idea and was glad that Calvin offered. She told some of her friends in class about studying with Calvin. They wanted to form a study group. Susan had to convince Calvin that a study group was a good idea. Susan told Calvin he needed to be more social. The science study group would be an excellent way to get to know other people. Calvin agreed, and they set up a regular meeting time and place.

The science study group seemed to help Calvin come out of his shell. He was the most knowledgeable person in the group. Talking and interacting with the members made him feel more comfortable. It seemed like Calvin was enjoying this group of people as much as his geological friends back home. Sometimes he would hang out around campus with different individuals in the study group.

Two months had passed since the study group was formed. People in the study group always sat together in the science class. At the beginning of this particular science class, they received grades from their third test. Immediately they started comparing papers. Everyone in the study group passed the test. Susan was still concerned because she had a low passing score. The only person she showed her score to was Calvin. Calvin saw the troubled look on Susan's face and said, "Don't worry about it. Your score will get higher."

Before the professor started the science lecture, he made an announcement for extra course credit. He said, "For those who want to receive extra credit in this class, we need volunteers for phase I of a Cryosleep Case Study. The participants will receive twenty extra points toward your overall test scores at the end of this class. Anyone interested in participating in this case study, please pick up a flyer on my desk after class." Susan was using her elbow to nudge Calvin as the professor was making the announcement. She was signaling to him that she wanted to participate in the case study. Susan saw this as a way to boost her grade. After the lecture, Susan took Calvin by the hand and went to the professor's desk. She grabbed two flyers and handed one to Calvin. "Calvin," Susan suggested, "let's volunteer for this experiment. These credits will help me boost my grade in this class". She quickly read the flyer and said, "there are only three requirements; to be currently enrolled in a science class, making passing grades, and attend the orientation."

Calvin replied, "I am interested in learning about cryosleep, so let's do it." Susan said, "There are several time periods to choose from to attend the orientation. Let's attend it together." "OK," Calvin responded, let's pick a time that will work out for the both of us."

On the day of the orientation, Susan and Calvin met in front of the building. They went in together. There were only four people, including Calvin and Susan attending the orientation. Susan said, "I thought it would be more people than this." "Me too," Calvin said. A tall older grey-haired gentleman entered the room. He pulled his chair around to face the four students. He started taking papers from his briefcase as he introduced himself. "My name is Professor Steve Taylor. I have been on the science faculty at this university for more than twenty years. How many of you are enrolled in a science class and have passing grades?" Calvin and Susan raised their hand. The other two people looked at each other and then stated that they were enrolled in a science class but do not have passing grades.

They thought by participating in this case study would assist in bringing their scores up. Professor Taylor explained that a passing grade was one of the requirements in participating in this case study. He shook their hands and thanked them for coming as they left the room.

Professor Taylor asked Calvin and Susan to introduce themselves. After briefly telling him about themselves, Professor Taylor began discussing the Cryosleep Case Study. “NASA awarded three universities contracts to perform a Cryosleep Case Study. I am proud to say we were one of the universities that received a contract. The university has chosen me to manage this case study. Have you heard of cryosleep?" Although Calvin had heard about cryosleep, both of them said no. "Cryosleep is the act of putting humans or animals in a suspended animated state through the use of drugs and placed in a cold chamber." The Professor handed Calvin and Susan a document. "This document gives a detailed definition of cryosleep. Each participant will be placed in a cryosleep state. They will then document any unusual experience they have after being put in the state. This information will assist in identifying what effects suspended animation will have on astronauts."

"Astronauts!" Calvin said in an excited tone. "Yes" Professor Taylor replied, "The United States wants to increase the distance of space travel. NASA wants to send our astronauts to planets that might take years to reach. They need a method that will allow an astronaut to be the same age when they reach a far off planet as they were when they left. We are conducting tests to determine if a cryosleep state will be the safest and effective way to put an astronaut to sleep and stop their biological clock, thereby eliminating the aging process." "Stopping the biological clock, are you serious?" Susan asked with a concerned look on her face. Professor Taylor replied, "The first four phases will focus only on putting the participants in a suspended sleep state. We are not testing stopping your biological clock. Don't worry." For phase I of the case study, each participant will be placed in an individual temperature controlled pod. We will use anesthesia to put them in a suspended state for twelve consecutive hours. During each phase of the study, the suspended time will increase by an additional 12 straight hours. This university has a contract to perform four phases. During the last phase, the participants are going to be suspended in the pod for 48 consecutive hours."

"Interesting!" Susan said as she looked at the clock on the wall. She had another class in one hour and did not want to miss it. Professor Taylor said, "You see how important this experiment is to the space program? I hope you decide to participate. It should be an enjoyable experience." He handed them another piece of paper. "This is the consent form you need to sign if you decide to participate in this study. There is a disclaimer and privacy statement at the bottom of this page. Please take your time and read all the information that I have given you." Professor Taylor gave them another piece of paper. "If you have any questions, here is my contact information. Feel free to ask me any questions you have about the Cryosleep Case Study. If you want to participate, drop off the consent forms at my office by the end of the month. We can then make arrangements to start the study". He stood up and shook their hands and thanked them for coming. Susan quickly stood up and rushed out the door, telling Calvin she must hurry not to be late for her next class. Calvin did not have another class to attend, so he strolled out the door. He was thinking about how interesting it would be to contribute to the space program. A smile came to his face as he walked toward his dormitory.

Once Calvin entered his room, the phone rang. It was a member of his science study group that wanted them to meet in the Student Union Building for dinner. Calvin confirmed the time and proceeded to take a shower. He was leaving his dorm room when his mother called. She had not heard from him for over a week. His mother asked, "What happened to the daily phone calls we use to receive from you?" "Oh, mother,"

Calvin replied, "I have been so busy with school. And now I am on my way to dinner at the Student Union with one of my friends." "I will not hold you up," his mother said. As she hung up the phone, she realized her son was beginning to enjoy campus life socializing with new friends. She looked at her husband and said, "Calvin is enjoying campus life. It seems like he has made new friends." Herman smiled. "Good for him." Darlene just hung her head down and walked away.

Chapter 7

The science study group was gathering at their usual place. The students were excited and started discussing the grade they received on their last test. One of the members said they like how Calvin broke down the subject matter because he made it understandable. Calvin smiled; he was feeling very confident. Susan interjected and started talking about the Cryosleep Case Study because she didn't want to discuss her test score. She told them she and Calvin decided to volunteer for the case study. Susan took out the document Professor Taylor had given them and read the definition of cryosleep. She made sure to tell the group the case study would help the NASA Space Program. Although they found the Cryosleep Case Study interesting, none of the members wanted to participate because their schedules were full.

Susan reminded Calvin that they had to sign the consent forms and select a case study date. She made a suggestion, "I like Sunday because that fits my schedule. I don't have any Monday morning classes." She pointed to the schedule and said, "This is the only Sunday date offered to perform the case study." Calvin was checking his calendar and realized it was the day after the paranormal convention he was attending with Alex. He looked up at Susan and said, "This is the day after the paranormal convention." "Paranormal!" a student said. Calvin explained he was attending the convention at the request of his roommate. "I believe in science, not in the paranormal," another member commented. Calvin remarked, "I am a skeptic too, but I didn't want my roommate to attend the convention alone." The group started talking about how they didn't

believe in the paranormal. In the middle of the conversation, Susan spoke up and said, "Calvin is such a good friend, although he doesn't believe in the paranormal, he didn't want his roommate to attend the convention alone how thoughtful." She wanted to emphasize the fact Calvin was a skeptic. It was important to Susan the science group didn't misunderstand him because they were the only friends Calvin socialized with on campus. The study group stopped talking about the paranormal and started turning pages in their books.

Calvin marked his calendar and said, "Susan, that date works for me. Let's sign the consent forms and take them to the Professor's office tomorrow." Susan nodded her head and said, "OK, let's meet at the Student Union." The study group proceeded to discuss the science assignment.

The next day Susan met Calvin at the Student Union. They had lunch and then took the consent forms to Professor Taylor's office. The Professor was in his office sitting behind his desk when they entered the room. He stood up and walked around his desk to greet them. They handed the Professor their consent forms and told him the date they selected for the study. The Professor smiled and marked it down on a document. He asked them if he could schedule the documentation sessions for the following three Sundays after being put into the cryosleep state. Susan responded, "how long are the documentation sessions?" "The sessions should only take one or two hours at the most." They checked their calendars and told him that those days are okay. Professor Taylor was on his way to the Cryosleep Test Lab. He offered to show them the lab and documentation room. Susan and Calvin were very excited to see the lab. They walked through the hall, asking the Professor various questions about the cryosleep test. Professor Taylor said, "I am glad you are so enthusiastic about participating in the case study. We need positive attitudes from our volunteers."

The Cryosleep Laboratory occupied the complete third floor of the building, and the test facility encompassed most of the space. Professor Taylor punched a code into the keypad located at the door of the lab. They walked in, and the Professor instructed them to have a seat in the lobby. They weren't allowed to enter the testing facilities but observe by looking through two large glass windows.

Observing from the window, they saw five pods covered in glass. Each pod contained wires connected to a monitor. There was a woman in a white lab coat sitting at what appeared to be a monitoring station. Calvin pointed at the lady and said, "that must be the doctor." Professor Taylor entered the lab and began speaking to the woman as she handed him a printout from the monitor. He read the printout and looked toward the pods. That is when Susan noticed there was a person in one of the pods. Susan said, "look, there is someone in there." Calvin looked at the pod, "sure is; I guess he is a test participant?" After Professor Taylor finished reading the printout, he patted the woman in the white coat on the shoulder then left the lab.

Professor Taylor entered the lobby and motioned for Calvin and Susan to follow him. They walked down the hall to a room located adjacent to the lab. The room had ten desks with a computer on each. Situated by the door were three printers. "This is the room to document any unusual experience you might have after being put in the cryosleep state," Professor Taylor said. Calvin asked, “How can we determine that?” The Professor replied, “All we need for you to do is document unusual events you experience in your life after the test. In other words, anything out of the ordinary. For example, if you start having nightmares, but you never had them before the test, document that experience. We have a Cryosleep Evaluation Team that will review your documentation and determine whether the experience is from the cryosleep test. Their evaluation might require you to come in and answer a series of detailed questions about the documented experience. The goal of the case study is to identify the effects cryosleep will have on astronauts. Therefore, documenting your events are vital to the Cryosleep Case Study. Any more questions?" The Professor asked as he prompted himself on the door, getting ready to answer them. Calvin and Susan looked at each other, hesitated for a second, and then said, “No." “If you do, you have my telephone number you can call me. The next step is for the doctor to review your medical records. If no health issues are preventing you from participating in the study, you're approved. I will inform you guys as soon as I have received your approval." Professor Taylor shook their hands, and they left.

Susan and Calvin were walking and talking about what they saw in the lab. Susan was feeling nervous. Seeing the person in the pod with wires attached to his head made her concerned. Calvin reassured her she would be fine. Instead of going back to their dorm, Calvin suggested grabbing some ice cream to lighten the mood. Susan smiled, and they both headed to the Student Union.

When Calvin returned to his dorm room, he was so excited about the Cryosleep Case Study, he began discussing the process with his roommate. He described the lab room and seeing a volunteer in the pod. Alex was very interested in the study and asked Calvin a lot of questions. Calvin said, "I will know more about it after we do phase one." Calvin handed him the document he received during orientation. Alex wanted to know could he keep it for a couple of days to read. Calvin said, "You can read it, but I need it back. I want to read it again before the test." "When is the test?" Alex asked. "The day after the paranormal convention. Do you still want me to attend it with you?" "Yes," replied Alex. "Just checking," Calvin said. They both laughed.

Calvin was enjoying campus life. He maintained average grades in all of his classes except for science. He excelled in science with one of the highest grade point averages in class. Calvin had adjusted to crowded places on campus as well. He was no longer anxious when entering a crowded building. He seemed not to notice crowds.

The members of the science study group introduced him to more people on campus. He attended soccer games and concerts with them. Calvin's circle of friends was growing. It was rare that he ate alone. If Calvin were sitting at a table eating at the Student Union, someone he knew would ask to join him. Calvin would also join one of his friends for lunch or dinner. While walking to his dorm from the Student Union, Calvin saw several people he knew and spoke to them. A smile came across his face because he realized the significant change from when he first arrived on campus. Now he knew people and was happily interacting with them.

Entering his dorm room, Calvin received a text from Professor Taylor stating that he was approved for the Cryosleep Case Study. He immediately called Susan to see whether the Professor gave her approval. Susan told him she just received the message of her acceptance. Calvin started talking about how excited he was to assist with the space program. Susan became nervous because she remembered the person in the pod. She did not want to think or talk about the case study. So, Susan cut the conversation short and told Calvin she had to study for a test.

When Calvin hung up the telephone, he noticed his roommate had left the cryosleep document on his bed. He thought what a great time to read this document again in more detail. After reading, Calvin decided to perform his due diligence by researching cryosleep online. He found articles that gave him a more in-depth understanding of cryosleep. He also read about how they accomplished the test. Initially scientists used pigs as test subjects because they have a gyrencephalic brain, and the white to gray matter ratio in their mind is almost equal to humans. Scientists used drugs and cold chambers to put pigs in a suspended cryosleep state. After waking up, the pigs exhibited abnormal behavior. It was the results of those tests that lead some scientists to conclude the cryosleep state would be dangerous for humans. They further stated, cryosleep might cause long term health risks to humans.

Calvin started to conjure up all types of scenarios in his mind. The more Calvin read about the test results on animals, the more stressed out he became. He was so upset that when Alex came into the room, he started ranting about the test. "Wait," Alex said, "What are you talking about?" Calvin replied, "I am talking about the cryosleep study, read this." Alex calmly sat down beside him and started reading. "Now look at this article," Calvin said as he went to another website. "Wait a minute," Alex said, "These are old articles. See, they wrote this one five years ago." Alex clicked back to the other article, "and this one, six years ago. You are not reading the latest findings. Don't internalize all that negative feedback. Find out what the scientists are saying about the latest findings. Technology has changed so much in the last few years. I am sure their opinions are different."

Calvin scanned the internet for the latest articles on the impact that cryosleep testing had on humans. The only information he could find were articles discussing the advancements of putting cryosleep subjects to sleep. He could not find any updated articles describing results from testing humans. Toward the end of the night, Alex noticed that Calvin was still upset, so he said, "if you have any questions, call Professor Taylor." Calvin replied in a disappointed tone, "OK, I will call tomorrow," and he closed his laptop.

For the next couple of weeks, Calvin routinely called Professor Taylor with questions. Although the Professor patiently answered his questions and assured him the test was safe, it did not ease Calvin's mind. He was still stressed out. Susan noticed that Calvin was worried. But, Calvin never revealed his concern about participating in the case study. He was determined to go through with the test because he knew Susan needed the grade. However, he repeatedly discussed his concerns with Alex. Calvin had worked himself up so much that Alex had to become the voice of reasoning.

On this particular night, Alex entered the dorm room to find Calvin complaining again, "if only I could see something in writing about the effects cryosleep has on humans." Alex began to show signs of frustration. He reminded Calvin that because putting humans in a suspended cryosleep state was new; he probably would not find that much information online. Using an irritated tone in his voice, Alex said, "I do not know what you are thinking, but you are aware the university would not put you in a position of being harmed." At this point, Calvin noticed Alex was getting tired of hearing him talk about his cryosleep concerns. Although Calvin was still anxious, he replied, "you are right."

They changed the subject and started talking about their plans for the next day. "Tomorrow is the day of the paranormal convention," Alex said. A gleam came into his eyes, "relax Calvin, we are going to have a good time tomorrow. I can hardly wait for the convention." Calvin stated, "I am relaxed. I'm going to bed early tonight because I must do laundry before we go." "I want to go to bed early tonight too!" Alex responded. Both of them prepared for bed and then turned out the light.

The next day Alex woke up in a happy mood. Calvin knew from the previous night's conversation he had with Alex he should not mention the Cryosleep Case Study. Both of them finished their tasks for the day and dressed for the convention. Their dress attire was a little more upscale than usual but still casual.

Walking to the car, Calvin asked, "What restaurant are we going to?" "I suggest we go to this seafood restaurant close to the convention. I heard the food there was good. Do you like seafood?" Alex asked. "Yes," said Calvin, "I have not eaten all day. I am so hungry."

It was a cheerful mood in the car. Alex turned the music up loud as they sung along. Alex commented, "We are acting like we have been penned up in a cage and just set free." Both of them laughed and continued to sing with the music.

The food at the restaurant was excellent. Calvin was so full that he felt a little sleepy. Alex noticed Calvin nodding and said, "Don't go to sleep now; we have not attended the convention yet. You can sleep on the way home." Alex gave him a bottle of water. Calvin took a sip, and it helped to wake him up.

Finding a parking space was difficult. After about fifteen minutes of trying to find parking on the street, Alex gave up and decided to park in a garage. All of the nearby garages were full. They had to park several blocks away from the convention. While walking, Calvin asked if Alex had the tickets. Alex reached in his pocket, and they were not there. They stopped, Alex checked his other pocket, and there they were. Both of them giggled and kept walking.

The convention hall was full of people. Vendors had set up tables to sell their merchandise. There were books, souvenirs, tee shirts, and all sorts of paranormal paraphernalia for sale. Alex was so excited that he just wandered off, going from table to table, looking at all of the merchandise. Calvin strolled behind Alex because he did not want to lose sight of him. Alex bought several items. He handed a bag to Calvin and said, "This is for you. Thanks for coming with me." Calvin looked into the bag; it was a bookmarker. The bookmarker had a picture of a creepy house entitled Amityville House of Horrors. Calvin thanked him, and they found their seats.

There were five speakers presenting information on their paranormal experience.

They used videos, slides, and audio recordings to provide their evidence of ghostly encounters. Every time a presenter came to the stage, Alex would nudge Calvin and whisper who they were. Calvin was surprised that Alex knew most of the presenters. During the break, Calvin asked Alex, "How do you know these people?" Alex replied, "I have been following the paranormal for over four years. Most of these presenters are popular in the paranormal community."

The paranormal television celebrities presented last. Their presentation consisted of video and audio evidence. Calvin was fascinated with the data they presented, especially the ghostly images they captured on video. Although Calvin was a skeptic, it was hard for him to dismiss some of the evidence the celebrities presented. The information displayed by the other presenters were not as convincing.

After leaving, Alex asked, "what did you think about the convention?" Calvin grinned, saying, "I was impressed with some of the evidence presented." Alex, with excitement in his eyes, asked, "Are you a believer now?" "No," replied Calvin, "but some of the video data was very compelling." Both of them chuckled.

Walking to the garage, Alex said, "I hope this took your mind off the Cryosleep Case Study you are participating in tomorrow. You seem a little more relaxed today." Calvin replied, "I appreciate you listening to me these last few weeks going on and on about my cryosleep concerns." "No problem," Alex said with a smile.

Calvin remarked, "I still feel a little anxious, but I don't want to display this nervousness tomorrow." "Try to practice some meditation that might help," Alex said, opening the door to the car. "Instead of meditation, I have a technique that will help." Calvin said. The friendly bond they had established made it comfortable for Calvin to share the coping strategy he learned from his therapist with Alex. "This technique has taught me to relax and let go of any anxiety that I might have." "Oh yeah, what is the technique because it may come in handy one day," Alex commented.

They sat down in the car and adjusted their seat belts. Calvin said, "Let's turn off the music for a minute." Alex turned the music off. "This is how it works. You close your eyes and imagine that you are putting your anxieties in a suitcase." "A suitcase?" Alex asked with a smile. "Yes, then imagine you are putting the suitcase on a plane. The plane is taking off going up, up above the clouds. Now the plane is out of sight. But the most important part is," Calvin said with a brief hesitation, "it will never land." Alex stated, "Basically, POOF, your anxiety vanished." "Exactly, never to land," Calvin said, "and that is the technique." Alex asked, "does this work?" "It has always worked for me; it helps me stay calm" Alex started driving out of the garage parking lot. Calvin reclined his seat, closed his eyes, and said, "So right now I am picturing putting this suitcase with the cryosleep anxiety on an airplane. The airplane is flying up into the clouds. I can't see it anymore." Calvin drifted off to sleep.

The traffic was all backed up. Alex had to inch his way through the traffic congestion to get to the highway. He turned the music to a low volume so he would not wakeup Calvin. Driving along, Alex noticed how beautiful the clouds were in the sky. He had never seen such unique, radiant colors. Alex thought to himself, maybe these clouds are a sign that this technique works. Glancing at the sky, he smiled and said, "OK, plane, don't land for Calvin's sake."

Chapter 8

Calvin tossed and turned all night. All of a sudden, he sat straight up in bed. Adjusting his eyes to the darkness, Calvin grabbed a bottle of water off the nightstand and took a drink. Quietly turning on the lamp, he checked the time. It was still early; Calvin turned off the light and laid back down. He tried to go back to sleep. While lying there in the stillness of the room, his mind started wandering. He began thinking of home and how he had not heard from his family for a while. I will call them tomorrow, he thought to himself. It took about thirty minutes until he finally drifted back to sleep.

The next morning Alex woke to the alarm going off, but Calvin didn't hear it. Alex had to wake him up. Calvin sat up in bed and stretched out his arms. He was feeling a little drained because of his restless night. His eyes glanced at the time, and quickly jumped up to shower. It was the day of the Cryosleep Case Study. He had to meet Susan in an hour at the Student

Union for breakfast. Calvin dressed and was hurrying out the door when Alex yelled, "Good luck man." "Thanks, he responded."

Susan was already sitting at the table when Calvin arrived. She noticed he looked exhausted. “Did you get any sleep last night?” "No," said Calvin, "can you believe I had a nightmare? I never had a nightmare in my life." Susan replied, "And we have not participated in the case study yet." Calvin smiled, saying, “I think it had something to do with that paranormal convention I attended yesterday.” "How was it? Are you a believer now?" she asked. "I enjoyed the time away from campus. The ghostly evidence they presented was interesting, but I am still a skeptic." They finished their breakfast and headed to the Cryosleep Lab.

Susan pushed the buzzer on by the Cryosleep Lab door. A voice over the intercom requested their names. After they identified themselves, they were buzzed into the lab. Professor Taylor greeted them with a smile and a handshake. “This is Veronica, the nurse that will assist you in preparing for the test today." Veronica shook their hands and said, "Follow me." She escorted them to a room where a lady with a lab coat was sitting at a desk.

"Good morning, my name is Doctor Limestone. I will be one of the attending physicians monitoring your test today. Have a seat." They sat down, and Doctor Limestone handed them a sheet of paper. "This is the consent form you need to sign, giving us permission to administer the anesthesia." Doctor Limestone explained how she would perform the test. In a matter-of-fact tone, she said, "We will be using anesthesia and a temperature control pod to keep you in a suspended cryosleep state. Nurse Veronica will place electrodes on your forehead and around your heart. The information from the electrodes will allow us to monitor your heart and brain digitally. If we see any signs of stress on your heart or brain, we will stop the test. There will be a doctor monitoring your condition for the whole twelve hours." She paused and asked, "Any questions?" Calvin and Susan replied, "No." She handed them another form to sign. “Then, please sign this form stating that I have clearly explained the test procedure to you.” They signed both documents and gave them back to Doctor Limestone. After Doctor Limestone left the room, Calvin and Susan were waiting for the next step. They started discussing the Doctor’s demeanor. “She seemed more serious than Professor Taylor or Veronica," Calvin said. "I noticed," Susan agreed. Doctor Limestone’s behavior made Susan and Calvin feel nervous.

Nurse Veronica came to the door and motioned them to follow her. They walked down the hall and stopped in front of two rooms. “These are your dressing rooms. Please change into these gowns and put all of your belongings into lockers located inside the room. I will wait for you out here," she instructed. Calvin was the last one to come out of the dressing room. He was tugging at his gown. "I hate these things," he commented. "Me too," Susan agreed.

Feeling a little nervous, they held hands, walking down the hall toward the lab. Susan could tell by the way Calvin gripped her hand that he was scared. “I know I am nervous about this test, but I thought you were not concerned," she stated. “Just a little nervous because this is a new experience for me. I will be fine.” Calvin reassured her.

Professor Taylor was standing in the lab as Nurse Veronica walked in. Calvin and Susan hesitated at the door. Come on in; we don't bite, the Professor said. Doctor Limestone was sitting at a long desk that contained several monitors. Please sit down, and let's go over one more thing, said Professor Taylor. "Did Doctor Limestone give you a thorough understanding of how we will conduct the test today?" They answered yes by nodding their heads. “Now is the time for you to back out if you don’t want to participate in this experiment. You need to know that we have tested four people before you. So far, none of them have experienced anything out of the ordinary. Now, do you still want to participate?”

They nodded yes. “OK, good, when you get into your pod, relax. Imagine you are an astronaut going out of space. You are traveling out of space just waiting to land.” “Interesting said Calvin, “this time we want to land Susan.” They both laughed.

Nurse Veronica led them to their pods. Susan was first to go into the pod. She was put in an upright standing position using two straps to hold her in place. Veronica placed the electrodes on her forehead and around her heart. She then placed Calvin in a pod and attached the electrodes on him. Professor Taylor’s voice came over the intercom and asked if they were comfortable. They gave him a thumbs up. An anesthesiologist administered the anesthesia and they drifted off to sleep.

Six hours had passed, and Dr. Limestone read the output of Susan's and Calvin's electrocardiogram. All of a sudden, Calvin’s monitor registered an abnormal signal. Dr. Limestone stood up to stop the test. But, before she could leave her desk, the alert returned to normal. She sat back down and documented the event into her log.

The twelve-hour test was over. Nurse Veronica woke Susan and Calvin up and led them out of the pod. “How do you feel?” she asked. “A little dizzy," said Calvin. "Me too," Susan agreed. "That's normal," she replied. "Sit here until you feel like getting dressed.” "I am glad this is over," Susan told Calvin. "It was not as bad as I thought," he replied. After a few minutes, they were ready to put on their clothes. After getting dressed, Nurse Veronica escorted them out of the lab and they left.

Leaving the test lab, Susan suggested they go to the coffee shop off-campus. The coffee shop was within walking distance to the campus. Susan wanted to walk to this coffee shop so her legs could get some exercise. They talked about the test all the way there. Calvin confessed to Susan about his anxiety before taking the test. Susan was surprised that he had worked himself in such a state without telling her.

They reached the coffee shop. It was very crowded, and the line was long. Calvin asked Susan to find them a table, and he would get the coffee. By the time Calvin ordered the coffee, Susan had found a table. Calvin paid for the coffee and looked back at the long line. All of a sudden, he stood still and blinked his eyes twice. Calvin saw a person in line that looked just like him. Not only did he look like him, but he had on the same clothes. In shock and amazement, he rushed to the table to tell Susan. Susan noticed something was wrong with Calvin as he approached the table. "Susan, Susan look, look," Calvin said. He had coffee in both of his hands. Calvin placed the cups down and started to point at the line. While pointing to the guy, his hand accidentally knocked Susan's coffee over into her lap. "Calvin, come on now, look what you have done!" Susan said. She stood up, and Calvin rushed over with napkins to help her clean the coffee off her clothes. Calvin was still excited and said, "Look over there; there is a guy in line who looks just like me." Susan glanced up at the line and said, "I don't see anyone that looks like you. What are you talking about?" Calvin glanced at the line, but the guy was gone. "He was there; he was even wearing the same outfit as me," he replied. "What, the same outfit?" She rolled her eyes and said, "Let's go, I need to change." Calvin was perplexed, "but I did see him!" "Sure," said Susan, "you must be tired. You need to get some rest. They walked back to campus. Susan said, "We will talk tomorrow."

Calvin was still confused when he entered his dorm room. Alex was studying. "Alex, guess what I saw?" "I don't know," Alex replied. "I saw a person that looked just like me." "Really," Alex said. "He was dressed in the same outfit as me, too." Alex asked, "Are you telling me you saw your doppelgänger?" "Doppelgänger, what is that?" asked Calvin. "A doppelgänger is your living double. It's believed in the paranormal world if you see your doppelgänger, it's a sign you will die," replied Alex. "What nonsense," I am just tired from the test. I am going to bed."

Calvin woke up the next day, refreshed. He and Alex walked to the Student Union Building for breakfast, discussing the Cryosleep Case Study. When they sat down at the table, Alex brought up the subject of the doppelgänger. Calvin immediately said, "You know I don't believe in the paranormal. I was just tired. There is no such thing as a doppelgänger." Alex insisted that doppelgängers exist. "There have been sightings throughout the centuries." "Yeah, right," Calvin said with a frown on his face. "Well, I hope you are right for your sake because it is a bad omen if you do see your doppelgänger," said Alex. "Now, you know I don't believe that!" Calvin responded. They finished breakfast and left for class.

The science study group was meeting. Susan began telling the students about the Cryosleep Case Study as Calvin joined them. Someone asked, "How do you guys feel?" Calvin answered, "so far so good. I am glad that it is over because I was a little nervous. But now I see there was nothing to be nervous about." "Me too." replied Susan, "the next step is to document anything strange that happens to us out of the ordinary." "That's it?" a member of the study group asked. Calvin took a deep breath and said, "Yeah, until phase two." The last student of the group entered the room. Calvin said, enough about the Cryosleep Case Study. Let's discuss this upcoming test.

The test they were studying for counted for twenty five percent of their science grade. Calvin knew that the group was depending on him to help them get a high score. Everyone seemed to be anxious as they started discussing the test topics. It was apparent that most of the members had not studied the subjects before coming to the meeting. They started asking Calvin question after question. As soon as Calvin answered one question, someone would ask him another. It was like a question and answer period instead of a group study. After thirty minutes of questioning, Calvin said, "Guys, you are wearing me out. I suggest we stop for now, and everyone needs to take a little more time to study on your own before we get together again."   Susan said,

"Good idea. Calvin is getting tired of all these questions, which is not fair to him. By the time we have our next study session, maybe we will be better prepared." They agreed to end the session.

Susan and Calvin left together. They were going to dinner in the Student Union. Walking to the building, Susan said, "I don't appreciate how aggressive some people acted toward you during the study session." "Yes, it became a little intense; that's the reason I stopped the discussion." "Good call; maybe the next time everyone will be prepared." They got their food and sat down at a table to eat. Halfway through their meal, Susan asked, "What were you trying to show me yesterday in the coffee shop?" "Oh, I thought I saw someone who looked like me." "Seeing someone who looked like you shouldn't have made you so upset." "But you don't understand; the person was also wearing the same outfit that I had on." "Oh, how unusual, how could that be?" "Alex called it a doppelgänger. Seeing one is supposed to be a bad omen." "Alex!" she said with a frown on her face. "I guess seeing a doppelgänger is a paranormal phenomenon." "Yes, it is." "So, Alex has you believing in the paranormal now?" She asked with a harsh tone. "No, I don't believe in that craziness." I was just tired." "Yes, that is what I'm thinking." Susan said in a more relaxed tone. Patting Calvin on the shoulder, she said, "You will be fine." They finished their food, hugged each other and started walking toward their dorm rooms.

It was such a beautiful day Calvin decided to take the long way to his dorm. The campus grounds were full of people as Calvin enjoyed the scenery. Strolling along, Calvin remembered that he had not called home for a couple of weeks. He sat down on a bench and called his sister. Cindy was happy to hear from her brother. She told him that their parents were wondering why he had not called. "Tell them I am busy studying but will call them tomorrow. I just have time for a quick hello." "Wait before you hang up the telephone. Did you hear about Jerry and Sarah?"

"No, I have not talked to any of my geological friends lately." "Well, Jerry and Sarah have set a wedding date, and she is pregnant." "Pregnant!" His eyes started filling up with tears. He quickly said goodbye and hung up the telephone. Calvin just sat there, staring into space. Feeling sad and hurt, he pulled up the old picture of them on his phone. Wiping the tears from his eyes, he pressed delete. "Oh well, that's that."

Calvin stood up and glanced around to see if anyone saw him crying. Students were everywhere on campus, and no one was paying him any attention. He started walking toward his dorm. Then from the corner of his eyes, he spotted someone who had on the same outfit as him. Glancing closer at the figure, he realized that the guy looked like him, too. "Doppelgänger, not again!" He couldn't believe his eyes. Coming to a complete stop, he rubbed his eyes, thinking it was just his imagination. Calvin closed his eyes, hoping when he opened them, the image would be gone. But, when his eyes opened, the doppelgänger was still there, walking across campus. Calvin started running toward him. Mumbling to himself, "I want to talk to this guy." Staying focused on the doppelgänger, Calvin was bumping into people trying to catch up to him. “Excuse me, excuse me.” He was keeping his sights on him. Calvin almost caught up to the figure when the doppelgänger turned the corner and went into the Administration Building.

Breathing hard, Calvin busted through the Administration Building's doors. He stood still and started looking around for him. The building was crowded, there were so many people walking through the halls. He stood in the middle of the hall. It put him in a position to watch the only two exits of the building. Ten minutes had passed, and there were no sign of the doppelgänger. He decided to call Alex because he needed help watching the exits so the doppelgänger would not getaway.

Alex answered the telephone. He briefed his friend on what had occurred and he needed his help. Alex was so excited about a chance to see a doppelgänger. He ran out of the dorm to the

Administration Building. It took him less than five minutes to arrive. "Are you positive you saw your doppelgänger again?" "Sure did; I followed him into this building. I have been keeping my eyes on both exits. I don't think he has left." "OK, Calvin, what do you want me to do?" Still looking around, Calvin said, “I will stand at the back exit, and you stand at the front. If you see him, give me a call." Alex headed to the front door and said, "OK, you do the same.”

An hour passed, and they had not seen the doppelgänger. Alex was growing tired, but he stayed focused, looking at every person exiting the building. He knew to witness such a paranormal event would be a chance of a lifetime. Alex planned on videoing the doppelgänger standing alongside Calvin and then posting it on the internet. He was rehearsing in his mind how he was going to pull this off. All of a sudden he spotted an image of a person that looked just like Calvin coming toward him. “That's him, that's him.” He quickly pulled out his phone to call Calvin. Alex was so nervous he almost forgot

Calvin's telephone number. "Come on, Calvin, answer the phone." The doppelgänger was getting closer and closer. Alex positioned himself to block the exit door. He knew he could not let the doppelgänger leave. If he could capture this paranormal phenomenon, he would become a star. The doppelgänger was almost standing face to face with Alex. "Hello Alex," Alex realized the figure was speaking into a telephone. The excitement left Alex's face. He stomped his foot, "oh man, this is you, Calvin. I thought you were the doppelgänger." Calvin lowered his head and said, "I am ready to leave. It has been over an hour. I believe he is gone." Feeling disappointed, Alex said, "OK, let's go."

Alex could tell that Calvin was upset. Calvin was thinking about how it was even possible to see his doppelgänger. He knew it was not a figment of his imagination. They strolled across campus to their dorm. Calvin almost walked into a tree because he was not paying attention to where he was going. Alex noticed and pulled him out of the way. "Calm down, Calvin." They stopped walking, giving Calvin time enough to gather himself. Calvin bent down and placed his hands on his knees. He took two deep breaths. "I am alright now." They continued to walk. With a sympathetic look in his eyes, Alex told Calvin, "I will help you sort this out. Don't worry."

Back in his dorm room, Calvin tried to study. He couldn't concentrate thinking about the news of Sarah's pregnancy and seeing the doppelgänger. Calvin decided to call Susan to tell her about the day's paranormal event. He knew talking to her may help him to relax. Susan answered the phone and was surprised it was Calvin. She knew Calvin had a test in one of his classes the next day and thought he would be studying. "Hello Calvin, how is your studying going?" "Not so well. I have had a rough time after I left you today." "What happened?" Calvin explained how he saw his doppelgänger again, and he followed him into the Administration Building. Susan did not comment. She was silent. "Susan, Susan, can you hear me?" "Yes, I am just trying to process what you are saying." "I got Alex to help me search for him, but we couldn't find the guy." "Alex! Now I get it," she said with an irritated tone. "Is he putting these crazy paranormal thoughts in your head?" "No, he is trying to help me figure this out." "You don't need his help because it's nothing to figure out. Just study for your test tomorrow. Can you do that?" "I guess so, but it is hard for me to concentrate." "Tell you what, I will meet you and Alex for breakfast tomorrow, and we will discuss this then. Put this out of your mind for tonight and study." "OK, I will try" they hung up the telephone, and Calvin started to study.

The next morning Susan joined Calvin and Alex for breakfast. They were already at the table when Susan sat down with her tray of food. "So, you are Alex." They shook hands. Susan had a strange look upon her face. "I want to know why you are filling my friend's head with all this paranormal mess." "What are you talking about? I am trying to help him figure this out." "He doesn't need your help. Thank you!" "Wait a minute, Susan, don't blame Alex. I did see my doppelgänger. I kept my eyes on him until he entered the Administration Building," Susan was still staring at Alex and said, "That's hard for me to believe. It all started when you attended that paranormal convention. Listening to all that stuff about ghosts has put those crazy thoughts into your head. Calvin, you are so gullible." Alex was becoming angry, he said in a harsh tone. "The convention had nothing to do with Calvin seeing his doppelgänger. Doppelgängers exist. People have documented them throughout history. Check it out!" Alex grabbed his phone and started to pull up the doppelgänger information. "I am not checking anything out. All this nonsense better stop. Doppelgängers do not exist, especially Calvin's" They were getting loud. Calvin interrupted them, "Stop fighting, you guys; I will figure this out." They stopped talking but continued to stare at each other.

Calvin quickly changed the subject. "Susan, I talked to my sister yesterday, and she told me Sarah and Jerry had set a wedding date." Susan knew them from high school. Her face had a puzzled expression when she said, “I was surprised to hear that they were dating.” “Well, guess what? Sarah is pregnant.” Saying those words out loud made Calvin a little teary-eyed. Alex noticed and asked, "Is she your ex-girlfriend?” “No, I had a crush on her, but we never dated.” Susan looked surprised, “I didn’t know that.” They continued to eat in silence. Susan finished eating and was waiting for Alex and Calvin.

She placed her hand on the side of her face as if she was thinking about something. She snapped her fingers and said, "Calvin, did you talk to your sister before or after you saw the doppelgänger?" "It was just after I hung up the phone." "OK, I got it, that news put you in such an emotional state which caused you to see things, like your doppelgänger. All you need to do is move on from that Sarah and Jerry situation, and you will be fine." Alex shook his head, disagreeing, and said, "I don't think that's what happened." Susan looked at him and rolled her eyes. "That is it, Calvin don't listen to Alex. I am glad I have figured it out. We don't need to discuss this anymore. Let's keep this doppelgänger situation between the three of us. I don't want anyone to think my friend is crazy." Calvin started to comment but decided not to say anything. There was already tension between Susan and Alex. He did not want to make it worse. So he said "OK," but Alex did not answer. They finished eating and left for class.

The next time Susan and Calvin met was the following Sunday. On the day of the Cryosleep Case Study's documentation session, they met for breakfast before going to the session. Calvin was the first to arrive. He sat down at the table and started watching people pass by. There was so much on his mind that he began to fall into deep thought. His concentration stopped when he saw Susan walking toward him, waving hello. A smile automatically came to his face as he waved back. Calvin was always glad to see Susan. Their friendship had blossomed, and he felt very comfortable around her. But today, there was something different about Susan. Walking closer to the table, he noticed how beautiful Susan looked. How strange, he thought, I never realized how attractive she was before now.

Calvin stood up and pulled out the chair for Susan. It was a ritual that he always performed for any lady that was sitting down at his table. Susan smiled and said, “Good morning; how are you feeling today?” “Good, how about you?” “I almost overslept this morning. But I am doing great.” Calvin kept staring at her. "Did you change your hairstyle or something?" "No, why?" Susan started looking at herself in the mirror. "I was just wondering. Let's get breakfast." They went through the line and got their food. It took them a while to find a table.

They finally sat down and started eating. The two were not talking much. At times during the meal, it was silent. Neither one of them wanted to bring up the subject of the doppelgänger. That was the gigantic elephant in the room. Susan finally asked, “Have you seen your doppelgänger again?” Calvin wanted to forget about the event. He started laughing, "No, I have not. I think you were right; the Jerry and Sarah situation got to me." Susan did not say anything as they continued to eat in silence. Calvin felt uncomfortable. To get back on track with their friendship, he knew that he had to clear the air. So he stopped eating, took her hand, looked in her eyes, and said, "Susan, I still don't believe in the paranormal. Don't worry about me. I will be fine." Calvin looked so sincere that she believed him. A smile came to her face. Calvin released her hand, and they continued to eat. Susan said, "I am glad to hear this. I was a little worried about you." "I know, but let's put this behind us." "OK," she said, wiping her forehead with her hands. "I am glad that's over. By the way, I want to apologize for how I treated Alex the other day. I hope he is not mad at me. I was just trying to protect you." "Alex is a good guy Susan. Don't be so hard on him." Susan looked at the clock. "It's time for us to go." They finished eating and rushed out the door.

They were the only two people in the documentation room. Professor Taylor came in and greeted them with a handshake and a smile. He handed them some papers. These are the instructions on how to document your events and how to save the file. Keep these instructions for your use throughout the three documentation sessions. Please read the instructions carefully. After five minutes, Professor Taylor asked, "Any questions? If not, you can start documenting your events. If you don't have an event, please make a note of that too."

Susan finished in about ten minutes. She wrote no abnormal events had occurred in her life. She printed out a copy. It took her a few minutes to figure out how to save the file. After saving the file, she left the room and sat in the hall, waiting for Calvin. In about an hour, Calvin came out of the room. Susan looked puzzled, "What took you so long?" "I had to document about the two times I saw my doppelgänger." "What! Why did you do that, Calvin?" Susan was upset. "I thought we agreed to keep that between the three of us." Susan knew it was a stigma associated with people believing in the paranormal. Now there is a record on file stating that he saw his doppelgänger. “You shouldn’t have put that in writing." "I had to because the Cryosleep Case Study requires for us to document any unusual experience." Looking frustrated, Susan said, "I just don't want people to label you as crazy.” “I want to help the space program. That means being completely honest about all experiences I have out of the ordinary.” Susan said with a disappointed look on her face, “Well, it is done now.”

Chapter 9

Calvin and Susan walked across campus in silence to their dorm. He knew she was upset with him for documenting his doppelgänger experiences. However, he thought it was necessary to stay true to the case study. Helping future astronauts was very important to him. Calvin tried to break the ice. “Are you studying for the science test?” She was talking slowly, “Yes, there were a few confusing topics. But, I will wait for the next study session to get clarification." Calvin could tell that she didn't want to talk by her tone and the answer she gave. So, for the rest of the walk, he stayed silent. He thought, she would get over it. When it was time for them to go their separate ways to their dorms, they waved goodbye.

Alex was sitting at his desk, studying when Calvin entered the room. “How did the documentation session go?” “OK, I guess. I wrote about my two doppelgänger experiences.” “Oh?” Alex replied with a surprising tone. “Now, don't get upset with me for documenting these events like Susan." Alex frowned, when Calvin mentioned Susan's name. "I am not upset. I understand that's the nature of the Cryosleep Case Study." "Exactly," Calvin said with a smile. He was relieved Alex understood that documenting those events was a necessary part of the study. With a confused look on his face, Calvin said, "I still have doubts about whether I saw the doppelgänger." "Sure, you saw your doppelgänger. Remember, during your last sighting, you said that you kept your eyes on him until he entered the Administration Building." "Yes, but I don't understand how it is possible." Alex turned around from his desk and looked at Calvin. "There are a lot of things that happen that we can't explain. You, science-minded people, believe there is a logical explanation for everything, but sometimes it's not. Like I have told you and Susan, people seeing their doppelgängers have been documented throughout history. Look it up." Alex turned back around to study.

Calvin logged into his computer and started researching doppelgängers. For about twenty minutes, the dorm room was silent. Then all of a sudden, Calvin said with a loud voice, "You are right; if you see your doppelgängers, it is a sign of death." Alex turned around and looked at Calvin. He could tell that Calvin was working himself up. "Calm down, Calvin. What are you reading?" "There are articles throughout the internet about how Abraham Lincoln saw his doppelgänger in the mirror on several occasions." "OK," Alex said calmly. "And you know what happened to him," Calvin said in an excited voice. Alex did not want to say anything that would contribute to upsetting Calvin. So in a calm voice, Alex said, "I just wanted you to research doppelgänger so you would know that seeing a doppelgänger is not so unusual. Don't start working yourself up like you did about participating in the cryosleep study." Then Alex turned back around, "I have a test tomorrow, and I need to study." It was Alex's way to stop talking about doppelgängers. Calvin took the hint and kept researching in silence.

All night Calvin tossed and turned in bed. He was dreaming about seeing his doppelgänger and holding a conversation with him. The dream was so disturbing that he woke up sweating. He drank some water and said to Alex, “I had a crazy dream about me having a face to face conversation with my doppelgänger last night.” “That sounds more like a nightmare to me. I would have been terrified.” “It did scare me.” “Well, you better stop reading all of those stories about doppelgängers on the internet. I believe it's getting to you." "No, I will be OK." Calvin went to the bathroom to get ready for breakfast. As he was brushing his teeth, Calvin began to stare at himself in the mirror. He still had the Abraham Lincoln doppelgänger story in the back of his mind. "Hurry up, Calvin," Alex shouted. That broke Calvin’s glance. He came out, and they went to breakfast.

Eating breakfast, Calvin casually mentioned to Alex that he was thinking about asking Susan out on a date. Alex turned up his nose. “Susan! She is cute and all that, but I am not a fan.” “You two just got off on the wrong foot. She is a nice person." Alex did not make another comment about Susan. He didn't want to discourage Calvin. Alex thought it would be a good idea for Calvin to start dating, even Susan. Dating might stop him from obsessing about those doppelgänger articles. "Follow your heart Calvin, ask her out." "Maybe I will, but I don't want to ruin our friendship." "Go for it; you will never know." Calvin started thinking about how he missed his chance with Sarah. "Alex, you are right. I am going to take a chance and ask her out." "Good, let me know what happens." They finished their breakfast and left for class.

The long look in the mirror that morning made Calvin realize he needed a haircut and a shave. He had neglected his appearance since he started living on campus. So, Calvin decided to spruce himself up before seeing Susan. He would meet her in a couple of days at the science study group session, and he wanted to look his best. After his last class that evening, he gathered up all his gift cards and caught the Hop and Ride Bus to the mall. The Hop and Ride Bus service was provided by the university for students and faculty use only. The buses followed routes from the university to locations within a thirty-mile radius.

He reached the mall without any problems and found his way to the barbershop. After he came from the barbershop, he decided to buy some new clothes. Calvin took his time selecting some shirts, pants, and shoes. Walking through the mall, he was thinking about how he would ask Susan out. It occurred to him, giving her a special greeting card could set the mood.

He found his way to the card store. It took him over ten minutes to find the right friendship card that expressed how he felt about Susan. Walking out of the card shop, Calvin noticed the time. The bus service would stop in about thirty minutes. So he made a mad dash to the bus stop. The bus was pulling up just as he reached the bus stop. He was glad to catch the bus because it was the last Hop and Ride Bus to campus. He got on the bus and looked around, there were no other passengers on the bus but him. It allowed Calvin to stretch out. He put his bags on the seat beside him and relaxed. A smile came to his face because he was proud of what he had accomplished at the mall.

Calvin was looking at the landscape as he rode down the street. He had never taken the time to venture outside the campus by himself until now. The bus driver stopped at a red light. Calvin started gathering his bags because he knew the bus was a few blocks away from campus. Calvin looked back out the window with bags in his hand to see how close they were to the north gate.

In the next lane to the left of him was another Hop and Ride Bus. The left turn signal turned green. That bus began to make the left turn into the south gate. As it passed, he noticed the side profile of the only person on the bus. How odd Calvin thought, this person is wearing the same shirt as me. Just then, the passenger turned around and looked directly at Calvin. With a smirk on his face he started waving to Calvin. Calvin couldn't believe his eyes. The passenger was his doppelgänger. Shocked and confused, Calvin jumped up and started pacing. He didn't know what to do. "No way," Calvin said out loud. The light turned green, and Calvin's bus proceeded to the north gate of the campus. "Sit down," the bus driver told Calvin. Calvin was so confused he didn't hear the bus driver. The bus driver had to tell him again in a loud tone. Calvin heard him this time and sat on the edge of the seat, not knowing what to do next. When the bus reached his stop, he got off and quickly ran to his dorm to tell Alex.

Alex was sitting at his desk studying when Calvin busted into their room. Exhausted from running from the bus stop, he said, "I just saw my doppelgänger again." Alex turned around, "What, where?" He jumped up and started putting on his shoes. Calvin was catching his breath. "He was on the Hop and Ride Bus going to the south gate." "Let's go find him because I want to video this." "It's too late. We would never be able to find him. The campus is too big." "Oh man, I was hoping to capture this paranormal experience and upload it to the internet.” Calvin sat down on his bed. He was silent for a couple of minutes. Alex could see that Calvin was agitated. "Don't be upset, Calvin; we will figure this out." Calvin sadly looked at Alex, "But Alex, this encounter was different." "How different?" "This time, he waved at me. As if he wanted me to see him." “Waved!” “Yes, with a sly grin on his face." "Wait a minute, are you telling me that your doppelgänger was interacting with you?" "Yes, that's what was so scary about this encounter." Alex looked puzzled, "I have never heard about a person interacting with their doppelgänger." "Now, I am confused more than ever.” Calvin said with a puzzled look on his face. Alex started doubting Calvin’s doppelgängers encounters. “Are you sure you saw him? Maybe you fell asleep on the bus, and it was a dream." Calvin could tell that Alex didn't believe him. "I know what I saw, and I was not asleep.” Alex went back to his desk to study, and Calvin started unpacking his shopping bags. After he finished,

Calvin began researching doppelgänger again on the internet.

The next morning while walking to breakfast, Alex commented on Calvin's new haircut. "You look much better with your hair cut in this style." Calvin was still upset and could not think of anything other than his experience with the doppelgänger. "You know Alex; the doppelgänger had this type of haircut too. How could that be?" Alex looked irritated. "Look, Calvin, you need to get your mind on your studies and stop thinking about this doppelgänger." "I know, Alex, but I can't get this out of my mind." Alex knew he had to do something to shake Calvin out of his doppelgänger obsession. He remembered the technique Calvin taught him. "Listen, Calvin" They stopped walking. "Tell you what, remember the technique you told me about?" "Technique" "Yes, the one you use to help to relieve your anxiety." "Yes, packing my anxiety in a suitcase." "Yes, that's the one. Well, it's time for you to stop with the doppelgänger sightings and start concentrating on your studies.

Finals are in a couple of weeks, and you need to put all your energy into your studies." "I know you are right, Alex." “So let’s try the technique now. Look up into the sky. See those beautiful clouds.” Calvin looked up. “Now close your eyes” Alex didn’t know whether this technique would work or not but knew he had to try something. "Right in the middle of the cloud, there is a perfect opening to send off your suitcase, never to land.” Calvin closed his eyes and went along with Alex’s suggestion. He realized Alex did not believe him based on this last doppelgänger episode and he was tired of hearing about it. So when Calvin opened his eyes, he said, "OK done, I should be fine now." They continued to breakfast.

Chapter 10

It is a couple of weeks before the Thanksgiving break. Calvin was going to his dorm to take a nap before dinner. Walking at a faster pace than usual, Calvin kept looking straight ahead. He did not want his eyes to wander around the campus grounds in fear of seeing his doppelgänger. He was feeling more relaxed after the never to land exercise conducted with Alex earlier that morning but still stayed guarded.

Alex was not in the room when he arrived. Calvin put away his books and stretched out on the bed, and went to sleep. He had been asleep for about an hour when Alex came into the room. Calvin's phone rang. The ringing of the telephone startled Calvin. He woke up and started reaching for the phone. In a groggy voice, he said, "Hello, hello, who is this?" The voice on the other end of the phone replied, "Calvin, this is your Aunt Barbara. Is everything alright?" "I'm OK; I was just half asleep. How are you doing,

Aunt Barbara?" "I am doing great. I called because I will be down in your area next week and want to take you out to dinner." Calvin knew he would be in the middle of exams during that time. Yet, he thought going to dinner with Aunt Barbara would be a nice break. Calvin marked down the date, did a little small talk, and then hung up.

By the time Calvin hung up the telephone, Alex was already studying. "Do you want to go for dinner?" Calvin asked. "No, I have already eaten. Exams start next week for me, and I must buckle down and study." "I am going to get some food and come back to study too. I have a science and speech exam next week. The science exam should not be hard. However, in the speech class, I must stand in front of the class and give a ten-minute speech." "A speech! Have you written one yet?" Alex asked, still looking at his computer screen. "Well, I am going to give a speech on how coal mining has affected the earth. That was my award-winning paper from high school." "Sounds great. I wish you good luck with that class. I would be nervous giving a speech in front of people." “I am a little nervous. It helps to know the subject matter. So all I have to do is practice, and I will be fine." Calvin walked out the door going to the Student Union to pick up dinner.

Calvin was walking at a fast pace. His eyes stayed focused straight ahead, going toward the Student Union. When he was almost at the building's door, someone called his name. "Calvin" He did not turn around in fear the voice might be his doppelgänger. "Calvin Clearwater," the voice shouted louder. At that point, he realized it was a woman's voice. He stopped, turned around, and saw Susan. "Oh, it's you," Calvin said with a smile. "Who did you think it was?" She asked. "Oh, I don't know. Are you going into the Student Union?" Calvin replied with a smile. "Yes, I am going to pick up a little food and go back to my room to study." "Me too." Walking in the building together, Susan noticed Calvin's new haircut. "I like your new hairstyle. It makes you look a little different." Calvin thought this would be the perfect time to ask Susan out. Just when he had gained his confidence to ask her out on a date, one of the science study group members came up. The three of them stood in the food line, discussing the science test. Tomorrow will be the last time the science study group will meet until after the Thanksgiving break. After purchasing their dinner, the three of them departed to their dorm. Waving goodbye, they said, “See you in the science study group tomorrow.” Walking back to the dorm, Calvin thought to himself what a missed opportunity to ask Susan out. I will ask her tomorrow after the science study group.

Calvin received a text message from Professor Taylor just as he entered his dorm. The Cryosleep Evaluation Team wants to meet with him after the documentation session. He replied with an “OK” and immediately started studying.

The next day before attending the science study group, Calvin took extra time to groom himself. He wanted to look dapper because he was asking Susan out. Calvin took out a new pair of pants and shirt from the closet and started removing the tags. Alex stopped studying and looked at him pulling the tags off the clothes. "What's going on?" Alex asked. "I am going to ask Susan out on a date today." "Good idea," Alex said and turned back around to his desk and continued to study.

The study session had already started when Calvin joined them. Everyone complimented him on his looks. Susan said, "Calvin, you look nice. Are you wearing new clothes?" “I decided to spruce up a little today." Everyone started to talk at once, discussing the test topic. Calvin said, "Let's conduct this session in an orderly fashion." Samuel, a member of the group, eagerly spoke up, beginning to ask multiple questions. “Wait, wait!” we should be discussing these subjects, someone said. That is when an argument pursued. Susan stood up and said with a yell, "Stop! I need this study session to pass this class. So if you don't mind, let’s discuss the test topics instead of each person asking questions. After each topic, if you still don't understand, then ask your questions." They looked at each other and shook their head in agreement, then proceeded to discuss the topics. At the end of the study session, everyone said good luck on the test and waved goodbye. Susan said to Calvin, "These people made this session so intense that I need a break. My head is hurting so I am going to the dorm to take a nap." Calvin knew that it was not an appropriate time to ask her out, so he said, "don't forget the documentation session on Sunday." They waved goodbye and departed.

Alex was still studying when Calvin entered the dorm room. Alex turned around and said with excitement, "Did you ask her out?" "No, it was not the right time. Our study session was crazy. The study group member's behavior gave Susan a headache. So she went to her dorm to go to sleep." "You missed your chance." "No, I am going to ask her Sunday before going to the documentation session." "Great, good luck." Alex was about to turn back around to study when Calvin asked. "Do you want to get some dinner? We can bring it back and study." "Sounds good; I am hungry. We can eat there because I need a break." Alex said as he put on his shoes. "Can I bring my speech and practice while we eat?" "Yes, I will be glad to critique your speech for you." Calvin grabbed papers from his desk and headed toward the door. "Calvin, you have your speech on paper?" "I feel better talking from papers." "OK, let's go." They headed to the Student Union.

They were sitting at the table eating their dinner when Alex asked, "Have you seen your doppelgänger since your bus encounter?" Shaking his head no, Calvin continued to eat without raising his head to look at Alex. "Did you tell Susan about this last doppelgänger sighting?" Calvin raised his head and said, "No, and I don't intend to." "I don't blame you because it sounded strange to me that your doppelgänger smiled and waved to you. I would not tell anyone that!" "I don't want to talk or think about it. I have just started to calm down from my last episode and want to keep it in the past." "I can understand that, so let's hear your speech." Calvin practiced his speech; they finished eating and left.

Walking back to the dorm, Calvin told Alex about the scheduled meeting with the Cryosleep Evaluation Team. Calvin surmised it was due to him documenting his two doppelgänger sightings. Alex looked concerned, "I thought you would be questioned about those two experiences. Wait until they hear about the latest doppelgänger incident. They are going to be surprised." "To stay true to the Cryosleep Case Study, I am going to document that event on Sunday." "Oh my!" Alex said with a frown. They both entered the room and started studying.

It was Sunday morning, and Calvin was already sitting at the table in the Student Union, waiting for Susan for breakfast. He was feeling confident and was determined to ask Susan out on a date. With card in hand, as soon as Susan sat down, he presented it to her. Susan looked surprised. "What is this for?" she asked. "Just read it." A smile came upon her face as she read the card. "Calvin, how thoughtful. I truly appreciate the kind gesture." "Susan, would you like to go to the harbor with me for lunch on Saturday?" Susan looked puzzled, "Are you asking me out on a date?" "Yes, I am," Calvin said with his chest sticking out. "Well, I will have taken most of my exams by Saturday, and it could be a good break. Yes, we can go to the harbor, but I am not sure if we should call it a date." "OK, let's not put a label on this now." They both smiled and stood in line for their breakfast. When they finished eating, they walked to the documentation room. Calvin told Susan not to wait on him after the session because he had to meet with the Cryosleep Evaluation Team. Susan was surprised, "I knew it was a mistake to document your doppelgänger encounters." "But as I told you, I must stay true to the case study." "I guess so." Calvin was glad he had to meet with the team after the documentation session. He knew it would take him a long time to document his last doppelgänger experience, and he didn't want Susan waiting on him.

After Susan finished her documentation session, she waved goodbye to Calvin and left. Shortly after Susan left, Professor Taylor came into the documentation room. He requested Calvin to go to a particular room after he had finished documenting for the evaluation meeting. Calvin finished writing his doppelgänger experience, saved the file, and walked down the hall to the meeting room.

The door was closed. Calvin knocked on the door and a person said, "Come in." Professor Taylor greeted him. "Come on in, Calvin, and close the door behind you." The Professor introduced him to the three members of the Cryosleep Evaluation Team. The team consisted of three doctors; a psychiatrist, psychologist, and medical doctor. Professor Taylor briefly described their role on the evaluation team. He stated that each evaluation team member would use their field of expertise to exam our volunteer's documentation of unusual experiences. Then collectively, they will determine whether being put in a suspended cryosleep state had any effect on the volunteers. After the Professor finished, the evaluation team started asking questions. They asked Calvin to give them a brief description of his life on campus so far.

After he was finished, Professor Taylor stated "You are the only volunteer that had abnormal experiences after being put in the cryosleep state." Calvin looked puzzled. The Professor continued, "Further data is required before we can conclude if your experience was due to this cryosleep study." Calvin had a frown on his face when he said, "I don't think this study has anything to do with it." Professor Taylor could tell that Calvin was upset. So he said in a calm voice, "We need to wait until we analyze the data from all three documentation sessions before we can determine the results. This is just the second documentation session. Today the evaluation team will be asking you detailed questions about your experiences you documented to date. Let's start the meeting."

"So, you are a freshman?" The psychologist asked in a factual voice. "Yes, I am," Calvin replied, and the psychologist started keeping notes. "You initially said you made daily calls home." "Yes, I was a little homesick at the start of the school year." "Uh, a little homesick for a couple of weeks." The psychologist stopped typing and asked, "Have you ever seen a therapist before coming to this university?" Calvin wanted to stay true to the case study, so he answered. "Yes, I became overwhelmed during high school taking exams. So my parents sent me to a couple of therapy sessions." "Oh," the psychologist said while typing on the computer. Those are all the questions I have.

The psychiatrist was the next person to ask Calvin questions. "Did you have any other paranormal experiences before being put in a cryosleep state?" Calvin talked about how he was a skeptic but went to a paranormal convention with his roommate. The psychiatrist looked puzzled, "And you didn't see the doppelgänger until after this convention?" "No, I did not," Calvin said with a stern voice. "My first sighting was a couple of hours after I finished the cryosleep test." "Hmm, I see. I have no more questions to ask."

The medical doctor discussed Calvin's electrocardiogram results. There was a two-second unusual reading during the cryosleep suspension. At that time, Doctor Limestone decided that this was just a glitch in the machine. Therefore, she continued with the test. The medical doctor stated that his heart had not been affected. But, suggested that Calvin see a neurologist to ensure there was no brain damage due to the cryosleep test. "Brain damage!" Calvin said in an excited voice. "You must be kidding." The doctor calmly said, "This is just as a precaution. I just pulled up your file and read your documentation you wrote today, and we have to make sure you are alright." Calvin felt insulted by the doctor's brain damage remark. He stood up and started to leave. Professor Taylor got up and put his hand on Calvin's shoulder. "Listen, Calvin, we have to make sure that cryosleep is not harmful. Remember, the goal is to help the space program." "I know

Professor Taylor, but I am fine." "Let's just get you checked out to be sure." Calvin looked sad as he said, "I will let you know if I will see a neurologist." "We will make the appointment for you, and we will charge it to the cryosleep study. Just let me know." "OK," said Calvin and he walked out.

Chapter 11

Calvin kept his usual fast pace back to the dorm. He was so mad about the Cryosleep Evaluation Team interview that he started murmuring to himself. "How dare they try to insinuate my brain is damaged!" His phone began to ring; Calvin stopped and answered the phone. It was Professor Taylor, "I was calling because I was worried about you." "You don't have to worry about me because I am fine," Calvin said in a harsh tone. "You left in such a hurry. I wanted to check on you." "In a hurry? I was not going to stay around and let them interrogate me any longer. It was more like an inquisition than an interview. They geared their whole questioning toward my mental stability. There is nothing wrong with me." Professor Taylor made a brief sigh and said, "I want you to calm down, Calvin. Please realize the team needed to conduct a preliminary analysis to determine if you were affected by the cryosleep test. They have not reached any conclusion yet." "Well, the way they were questioning me, it seemed like they had already drawn their conclusion." "The Cryosleep Evaluation Team must do their job. Just relax; this is part of the process. You understand, don't you, Calvin?" Calvin did not reply. Professor Taylor knew Calvin was upset, so he ended the conversation by saying: "The next step is a brain scan." "I am not going to see a neurologist." Calvin said with a harsh tone. "Seeing a neurologist is a vital part of the analysis. Please reconsider, Calvin." Calvin stayed silent. Professor Taylor didn't push the suggestion any further. "Give me a call if you change your mind, and I will schedule the appointment for you." They hung up the phone, and Calvin proceeded to his dorm.

When Calvin entered the dorm room, Alex was looking at a television program. "How was the interview?" "It was not an interview; it was an interrogation. Similar to being questioned by the police." Alex heard a sharp tone in Calvin's voice. His voice was so harsh it made him glance up at Calvin. Alex noticed a look in Calvin's eyes that he had never seen before. The look of anger. “What do you mean, Calvin?" The majority of the questions were about something being wrong with me, and now they want me to see a neurologist.” “Don’t be so upset. They have to do their job.” “Their job is to conduct an impartial interview. But it seems like they had already concluded that my brain is damaged.” Alex wanted to calm his friend down. He knew the next couple of weeks were exam time, and Calvin needed to study. So he said, "Listen, don't be concerned about this cryosleep experiment. Exams are coming up, and studying should be your priority." Calvin was sitting at his desk at this time with his hands folded. He did not answer Alex. "Calvin, did you hear me?" Calvin looked at him, still not saying a word. “This is just a volunteer project. If you don’t want to participate anymore, you don’t have to.” Alex couldn’t tell if he was getting through to Calvin. He knew how worked up Calvin could get. So Alex wanted to change the mood. He thought by suggesting something fun to do might snap

Calvin back to his regular self. Alex said, “Listen, I have an idea. Exams will be over in a couple of weeks, and we will be going home for Thanksgiving break. After exams, let's go off campus to celebrate before we go home. I will make all the arrangements. Forget about that stupid Cryosleep Case Study and concentrate on finishing exams. We can then go out and have some fun.” Calvin’s face started to relax, “Going off campus to celebrate is a good idea, Alex. In a couple of weeks, I will be going home.” “Yes, and you can put this all behind you.” Calvin reached for the phone, “I need to call my parents and make arrangements for them to pick me up.” Alex continued to watch television while Calvin called his father. Herman was glad to hear from him. They chatted for a short time then made arrangements. Calvin noted everything on his calendar.

After he hung up the telephone, Alex could tell Calvin was almost back to his regular self. "Are you hungry, Calvin?" "Yes, I am Alex." Alex turned off the television and suggested going to the Student Union. Once he mentioned the Student Union Building, it reminded Calvin of what happened at breakfast that morning. A big smile came to Calvin's face when he said, "I asked Susan out this morning, and she said, yes!" Alex was glad the conversation had changed. "Well, good, Calvin. When are you going out?" "Saturday for lunch." "Let me know how it goes." They both continued out of the door.

On Monday morning, Calvin woke up feeling refreshed. He had promised himself the night before to block all the cryosleep evaluation and doppelgänger incidents out of his mind. Calvin had a full schedule this week. Today was his science exam. His speech exam was on Friday, the same day as Aunt Barbara's visit. The date with Susan was scheduled for Saturday. In the next two weeks, it was essential for him to study to pass his exams. With a renewed outlook, Calvin left for breakfast with Alex.

Calvin entered the science class and sat with the members of the science study group.

Everyone was chatting about the exam. They started asking him last-minute questions. He was glad when Susan entered because everyone seemed to stop asking him questions. Susan sat next to him and greeted him with a hug. Calvin could tell she was nervous. He held her hand and said, "Don't worry, you will do fine." "I hope so." "Good luck Susan." They relaxed and waited to take the exam.

Calvin was the first one to finish taking the exam. He waved goodbye to Susan and left. Walking to his dorm, the memory of his doppelgänger entered into his mind. Picking up his pace, he walked faster and kept looking straight ahead. After he reached his dorm room, he said, "Good, the coast is clear." “What did you say?” Alex asked. “Oh nothing, I must start studying for next week’s exams.” “I am off now to take my exam.” Alex said. “Good luck Alex.”

The dorm room was quiet while Calvin began studying for his calculus exam. Calculus was not one of his best subjects, but he had been able to maintain a passing grade. It was Calvin’s goal to pull up this grade by making a high score on the test. He tried to understand the various functions but became confused. He was still struggling when Alex came into the room. Alex could tell that Calvin was frustrated. "How is it going, Calvin?" "I'm having problems with these calculus functions." "Relax, why don't you go to the math lab for help?" "I like to try and figure it out for myself." "Why? There is nothing wrong with asking for help. Let's go there before it closes. We can get dinner after you finish." Calvin did not feel comfortable asking for help. But he knew Alex was right, so he said, "OK, let's go."

On Friday morning, Calvin woke up feeling overwhelmed. Studying for exams this week proved to be a bit challenging. Several times he had to visit the math lab for help. He also had problems studying for his remaining classes. Recognizing his anxiety, Calvin sat on the edge of the bed, closed his eyes, and performed the Never to Land Technique. It seemed to calm him down.

Calvin was still grooming in the bathroom when Alex asked, "Are you ready for breakfast?" "No, go ahead, I am not eating breakfast this morning." "OK, good luck." He took the extra time to shave and put on a new shirt. Calvin wanted to look his best, giving his speech in front of the class. Staring in the mirror, Calvin practiced his speech one last time before he left for class.

The speech class was held in a large lecture hall. It was a different room than his original class. The professor intended to have all the students give their speeches in a larger setting. Calvin was the second to come to the podium. With papers in hand, he introduced himself. Calvin began to speak, the lecture hall door opened. The squeaking of the door made him look up. Calvin watched as a guy entered wearing a shirt just like his. The figure stood in front of the door with his arms folded. Calvin was startled as he stared at the guy. Blinking his eyes twice, he realized that this was his doppelgänger. The doppelgänger waved to Calvin. Since everyone was facing the podium, no one saw him but Calvin. In a nervous state, Calvin dropped his papers, and they fell to the floor. He quickly bent down to pick them up. About the time Calvin stood back up, he looked again, and the doppelgänger was gone. Calvin became noticeably nervous. Realizing his grade was on the line, Calvin arranged his papers, cleared his throat, focused, and gave his speech. After his speech, he sat down but could not concentrate on the other student's speeches. He started rocking back and forth in a nervous twitch, thinking to himself, how could this be? I thought this was over.

After class, he ran to the north gate to wait on Aunt Barbara. Calvin had made arrangements to meet her there because it was easy to find. He didn't want to see the doppelgänger again, so he did not let his eyes wander. Standing at the north gate, Calvin was having a complete meltdown; he needed to talk to someone. He started to call Alex but hung up. Calvin knew Alex wouldn't believe him. He could never discuss this with

Susan because it might upset her. He never told her about the bus encounter. Calvin decided to keep this incident to himself. Pacing back and forth, waiting for Aunt Barbara, he was very nervous. "Calvin," he heard someone calling his name. Calvin did not turn around. Then someone touched his shoulders. He almost jumped out of his skin. It was a member of the science study group. "I'm sorry if I scared you. How do you think you did on your science exam?" Calvin was relieved. Still looking ahead, he replied, "I think I passed it." "Me too, I am going to the coffee shop. Do you want to join me?" "No thanks, I am waiting for someone." "OK," he walked away.

Aunt Barbara pulled up with her music playing. Calvin hurried into the car and fastened his seatbelt without speaking. "Well, hello, Calvin, why are you in such a hurry?" "Oh, I am not hurrying. I am just ready to eat." Aunt Barbara noticed the nervous look upon his face. Driving to the restaurant, she tried to make small talk, but Calvin was not responding. He was thinking about seeing his doppelgänger in the speech class. Calvin started rocking back and forth. Aunt Barbara felt uncomfortable. “What is going on, Calvin?" He did not reply. "Calvin, Calvin!” He snapped out of his daze, "Yes, Aunt Barbara." "What is your problem?” "Nothing, I was just thinking about something," Calvin replied. “Thinking about what?” He hesitated, “it’s a long story.” “I have time.” They arrived at the restaurant. Aunt Barbara parked the car and looked at Calvin and said, “We will sit right here until you are finished telling me what’s going on.”

Aunt Barbara unbuckled her seatbelt and let down the windows. Calvin was still silent. "Calvin, you know you can tell me anything. I will not judge you." "Well, this is weird." "I can handle weird. It might help you feel better to get it off your chest." Calvin thought about it for a second, then asked her, "Do you know the definition of a doppelgänger?" "Yes, I do." He was surprised that she knew the definition, it helped him feel better about telling his experience. He unbuckled his seatbelt, stretched out his legs, took a deep breath, and began to summarize the whole story. Calvin started with the Cryosleep Case Study and ended with today’s sighting of his doppelgänger. After he finished, he exhaled and said, "I am glad I told you. I wanted to talk to someone," Calvin began to relax. Aunt Barbara noticed, “Now don’t you feel better?” "Yes, I do." She smiled, “I just need time to process this before I can give you my feedback. But for now, let's go in to eat." They closed the car door and walked toward the restaurant.

Aunt Barbara wanted to change the subject. She said, “I chose this restaurant Calvin because I heard their meatloaf is good.” “Meatloaf is one of my favorite.” “I know it is; the meatloaf served here might not be as good as your mother’s, but we will see." The waiter showed them to their table. They placed their order. “Tell me about your life on campus. Have you made any friends?” Calvin’s face started to light up as he talked about Susan and Alex. He even mentioned going out tomorrow with Susan. Aunt Barbara was glad to hear Calvin had made close friends. She knew it was hard for Calvin to open up to people. After they finished, they walked to the car.

Driving back to the university, Aunt Barbara asked, “What do your friends think of this whole doppelgänger situation?” "I told them part of the story, but I prefer to keep some of the doppelgänger sighting to myself." “Your friends can be a good support system. I believe you can trust telling Susan and Alex the whole story.” “I don’t know about that.” “You felt better telling me. It even seemed to calm you down. Telling your friends might make this situation less stressful for you. Have you told your parents?” “No," “Really? Calvin, you should.” “You should think about telling them.”

Aunt Barbara parked at the north gate of the university to let Calvin out. Calvin unbuckled his seatbelt and began to open the car door. "Wait a minute, Calvin. I have something for you." She reached into her pocketbook and pulled out her rosary, and handed it to him. "Aunt Barbara, you know I am not religious." Calvin said with a smile.

"I am not either, but I have had several occasions in my life where I needed a blessing." "Seriously?" Calvin surprisingly asked. "Yes, just remember there are no atheists in foxholes." Calvin started laughing. "When you see your doppelgänger again, hold this rosary, close your eyes and say a silent prayer." "Thank you, and I will." Calvin stepped out of the car, closed the door, and started walking toward the gate. Before Aunt Barbara pulled off, she rolled the window down and shouted to Calvin, "I believe you, Calvin." Calvin waved goodbye with a smile and started walking at a fast pace toward his dorm.

Chapter 12

The smile on Calvin's face slowly disappeared as he walked toward his dorm. Walking faster and faster, he grew increasingly paranoid. By the time Calvin entered his dorm room, he had become utterly exhausted. Alex was still up studying, "How did you do in your speech class?" Calvin hesitated and then said, "OK." "Did you enjoy your dinner with your Aunt Barbara?" "Yes, it was a pleasant visit." Alex was confused because he noticed Calvin's stressed look. "Then what is wrong with you, Calvin? You seem upset. What happened?" Calvin wanted to tell Alex about his doppelgänger experience but decided not to. "I am tired, and I just need some rest."

It was early in the evening when Calvin decided to go to bed. He tossed and turned in bed for about an hour. Calvin couldn't sleep, so he got up to drink some water. Alex was still awake studying. Calvin sat on the side of the bed and put his face in his hands. He was thinking about his doppelgänger sighting. He needed to get some rest. Calvin decided to tell Alex about the sighting because he thought it would help him to feel better. Calvin slowly removed his hands from his face, sipped some water, and said, "Alex let me tell you what happened to me today." Alex closed his laptop and looked at Calvin. Calvin started to talk but hesitated. "OK, tell me what happened, Calvin. I have finished studying, and I am all ears." Calvin remained silent for a second and then said, "Well, Alex, my doppelgänger came into my speech class today and waved to me. It happened just as I was about to give my speech." Alex looked surprised, "Oh, Calvin, are you sure?" "Yes, I am. I didn't mention it when I came in because I knew you wouldn't believe me." Alex didn't want to add to Calvin's frustration. So he thought for a second and said, "It isn't that I don't believe you. I just never heard of an interacting doppelgänger." Calvin said with a frustrated tone, "Well, I never heard of a doppelgänger before either, but yet here I am, right in the middle of a paranormal situation. Imagine that!" Alex smiled, walked over, patted Calvin on the shoulders, and sat back down. "You made your point, Calvin; there are a lot of things I haven't heard of or experienced. However, that doesn't mean they don't exist." "Exactly! This whole situation has gotten me feeling like I am losing my mind." "You are not losing your mind, Calvin. Anyone that has seen their doppelgänger would be shook up. Tell you what, let's get a good night's sleep and discuss this tomorrow. Don't you have a date with Susan tomorrow?" Calvin smiled, "Yes, we are going to the harbor." "That sounds like fun. It would be best if you got a goodnight's sleep. So relax for now. I will help you figure this out tomorrow." Calvin went back to bed, feeling a little relieved because of the support Alex showed. He thought to himself, Aunt Barbara was right. I will tell my parents tomorrow.

The next morning Calvin woke up still feeling anxious. He showered, put on his clothes, and waited for Alex to go to breakfast. While waiting, Calvin decided to call his parents and tell them about the whole doppelgänger situation. He knew his parents would be upset, so Calvin practiced using a calm voice before contacting them. His father cheerfully answered the phone. "Hello son, how is it going?" "It's going fine. I have something to tell you and mom." "Wait, let me get her. Honey, Calvin is on the phone. He has something to tell us." Darlene hurried to the phone, "Hello Calvin; we can't wait for you to come home for Thanksgiving." "Yes, mom, I can't wait either. I called because there is something weird going on that you need to know about." "Weird?" Darlene asked in a stressed voice. "Calm down, mom." "Yes, Darlene, let the boy tell you what's going on. Go ahead, Calvin." "Have you heard of cryosleep?" They both said no. "Well, cryosleep is similar to putting a human into a medical induced torpor state. You know, similar to animals hibernating." Herman said, "OK, we get it." Calvin began to summarize the chain of events that led him to call them. Herman said, "So you saw this so-called doppelgänger several times?" "Yes, dad, and it wasn't a figment of my imagination." Herman tried to remain calm, "Son, could it be you are stressing yourself out because of exams. You know how it was in high school. We sent you to a therapist to overcome the stress." Darlene was livid; she interjected in a loud tone, "No! Herman, I think it was that cryosleep test. Who gave them permission to put you in a cryosleep state?" Calvin said in a stern voice, "I did, mom. I told you it was for extra credit." Herman said, "Everybody calm down. Calvin, we will be there in a couple of weeks. Do you want us to come before then?" "No, dad, next week I have several exams. I can handle this situation." "Good son, be strong. When we come down, we need to meet with Professor Taylor to discuss this Cryosleep Case Study. Please set up the meeting." His mother said, "Yes, we will be there to straighten this out. Calvin, don't worry." "I won't, mother." With a calm voice, Herman said, "What do you need from us to help you through your exams next week?" "Just a lending ear." "We are here for you, Calvin, you know that." "Yes, I know, dad." Herman said, "By the way, son, we will take you to our doctor for an examination. Don’t go to their neurologist." Darlene shouted, "Yes, because we might have to sue that university if anything is wrong." "Oh, Darlene, nothing is wrong with him. Calvin, study for your exams and don't let this bother you. We will see you soon." "OK, I am going to breakfast with Alex now. Goodbye," They hung up.

Calvin breathed a sigh of relief, just as Alex mentioned, "I am ready for breakfast." They left for the Student Union Building. They were at the table eating when Alex said, "I thought about your doppelgänger sighting; this is what you should do." Calvin stopped eating, listening intensely. "Ignore it." "Ignore it," Calvin replied in a strained voice. "Yes, just for now because you have to pass your exams next week." Calvin was silent. "If you let these sightings dominate your thoughts, you might not pass your exams. So if you see your doppelgänger before you finish your exams, ignore him. Don't give him a second thought." Alex said with a serious tone. "I am not to pay him any attention!" "Yes, act like he doesn't exist and don't worry about it."   Calvin thought about it for a second and said, "Alex, I think that is a good strategy." They both smiled and finished their breakfast.

Calvin was ready for his luncheon date with Susan. He had arranged for a car to pick them up at the north gate. Walking through campus was still challenging, but his eyes stayed focus in front of him. Susan was already at the north gate when he arrived. They greeted each other with a smile and a hug. She noticed Calvin looked stressed, "What is going on?" she asked. "Oh, I had a tough week. I will tell you about it when we get to the harbor." Susan was curious, "Can you tell me now." Just then the car pulled up. They got in and remained silent all the way there. When they arrived, they got out of the vehicle. Susan pointed and said, "Look, there are two chairs by the water, let's sit down. I want to enjoy this weather. It's not often we get away from campus." They sat down, but Calvin couldn't seem to relax. "Tell me what happened this week, Calvin. You seem nervous." With an exhausted look, Calvin took Susan's hand and said, "I haven’t told you the whole story about my doppelgänger sightings." Susan started to say something but stopped. "I know you don't believe that I saw my doppelgänger, but let me tell you about this anyway." Calvin told her about the last two sightings and braced for her reaction." Susan took a moment to respond, "Calvin, it seems like you are in distress over these sightings. As a friend, I am going to keep an open mind and work with you through this. There is a valid explanation, and we just haven’t figured it out yet." Calvin was surprised at the compassion shown toward him. "I am glad you didn’t get upset." Susan smiled to lighten the mood. "Now isn’t the time to flip out over this paranormal mess. We both need to stay calm and figure out a solution. More importantly, you need to stay focused and pass your exams next week." "You are right; Alex said the same thing this morning." "Alex!" Susan said with a frown on her face. "Susan, Alex is a good friend. He has been helpful throughout this whole semester. We are going out to celebrate next weekend." "Oh yeah," "I would like it if both of you would get along. After all, you two are my best friends." "Tell you what, Calvin, if getting along with Alex will make you happy, then I will come to the celebration next weekend. I can get to know Alex a little better in a different environment. Just call me with the details." Calvin thought to himself, I don't know if this is a good idea, but he said, "OK, I will call you and let you know." "For now, Calvin, just relax." "Susan, it is becoming increasingly difficult for me to concentrate while studying." Susan thought for a second. She looked up and said, "Hey, Calvin, they have the Wheel that looks over the harbor. Let's go on it; I have an idea that might help you focus." Calvin was curious but didn't say anything. He just stood up and walked with her to the Wheel.

The line was short. They immediately sat down, and the attendant buckled their safety belts. The Wheel was slowly moving higher, allowing them to see the water and the complete harbor's scenic view. When they reached the top, the Wheel stopped. It was the routine of the Wheel ride. It gave their customers a chance to get a better view of the harbor. Susan took this opportunity to tell Calvin her idea about calming down, "Calvin remember the stress reliever technique you taught me?" Calvin looked puzzled, "The Never to Land Technique." "Yes, that is the one." She held his hand, "Now close your eyes and send this doppelgänger situation into these clouds, never to land." Calvin looked up to the sky, smiled, and closed his eyes. When he opened them, they were halfway back down to the ground. "Susan, I think that did the trick." "Good, now you can focus on your exams." Calvin laughed and said, “Let's go, I am glad to have you as my friend." Susan smiled and said, "I am hungry. Let's get something to eat." They walked hand in hand to the restaurant with a smile on their faces.

Chapter 13

Alex wasn't in the room when Calvin came back. Calvin immediately sat at his desk and turned on the laptop to start studying. Susan and Alex had given him the motivation he needed to concentrate on studying. Before he began, Calvin reached into his pocket and pulled out the rosary beads Aunt Barbara had given him. Rosary clinched in hand, Calvin looked up to the sky, said "never to land," then began studying.

Calvin had finished studying when Alex came into the dorm room. They chatted about his date with Susan. He told Alex that Susan wanted to go out to celebrate with them. Although Alex wasn't happy about her joining them, he didn't want to add to Calvin's stress. So Alex smiled and told him it was alright for her to come. Calvin looked relieved and asked, "Have you eaten dinner?" "No, I have not." "Let's go and eat." "OK, Calvin, I'm hungry." They left for the Student Union food court.

The next morning Calvin woke up late. He had to meet Susan for breakfast before the last case study documentation session. He rushed into the food court at the Student Union. Susan was already at the table. "You are running late, Calvin. We can grab a sandwich and eat as we walk to the session." "OK, let's go."

They entered the documentation room. Professor Taylor greeted them with a smile. "Good Morning; after this documentation session, you have completed phase one of the Cryosleep Case Study." He handed each of them a letter enclosed in a picture frame. Professor Taylor said in an official tone, "The director of the NASA Space Program gives this to you in appreciation of your assistance to the space program." They looked at the letter started to smile. Each letter addressed the volunteers by their name. It was typed on NASA's official letterhead and signed by the director of the program. "Thank you," Susan and Calvin chanted. "Now you must document your last experience, and the study is complete," Professor Taylor said.

They logged into the computer and started to document. Professor Taylor walked over to Calvin, pulled up a chair, and sat down. He asked, "Have you reconsidered going to the neurologist?" Calvin said politely, "No, I am going to my family doctor. My parents have scheduled the appointment during the Thanksgiving break." "Will your doctor share the information with us?" "I'm not sure you need to discuss this with my parents. They want to meet with you when they pick me up next weekend." "Call me next week, and we can coordinate a time." Professor Taylor said. "OK," Calvin replied and started documenting, the Professor left.

Calvin continued to document the doppelgänger encounter that occurred in the speech class. When Susan finished her documentation, she waved goodbye. The NASA appreciation letter gave Calvin a sense of pride. He wanted to take his time to thoroughly document the incident because he had a renewed belief in the Cryosleep Case Study. Calvin finished documenting and left the room feeling a little more relaxed because the case study was over. As he turned the corner walking to the elevator, he was surprised to see Susan waiting for him. They both smiled, "Susan, I thought you were gone." Susan started laughing. "I fooled you." "You sure did." She handed him a greeting card. Calvin read it and became a little teary-eyed. Susan said, "I know you are having a rough time. I thought this card would lift your spirits." "I appreciate this, Susan." Susan held his hand and said, "No, Calvin, the appreciation goes to you. I know you volunteered for this case study because of me. You didn't need the credits." "Well, yes, you are right. But that is what friends do, help each other out." "The card is just to say thank you for being such a good friend." Entering the elevator, Calvin said with a smile, "Susan, this has been an awesome experience despite all the craziness." "It sure was." They left the building, laughing and talking. Bidding each other goodbye, Susan smiled, "Good luck on your exams, Calvin." "You too, Susan. I will see you on Friday night when we go out to celebrate." They went their separate ways to their dorms.

Calvin's week was hectic because he had to take three exams. Studying was not as challenging for him this week. The Never to Land Technique and the support of his parents and friends helped him through it. After each exam, Calvin breathed a sigh of relief. By the time he finished exams on Thursday, he was so excited that he went to bed early and slept until the next morning.

Calvin woke up Friday feeling very happy. He was ready to celebrate Thanksgiving break, and looking forward to going home. Calvin called his father to give him an update on his exams and to schedule the time of pick up. He also told his father the time on Saturday to meet with the Professor. Herman was glad his son finished his exam without an incident. Calvin hung up and went to the food court in the Student Union. Alex couldn't go with him because he was finishing an assignment to turn in by noon.

Walking across campus, Calvin didn't feel as intimidated. His eyes stayed focused ahead, but his pace was slower. Halfway to the Student Union building, he patted his pocket to make sure the rosary was there. Feeling the rosary, Calvin became more relaxed. When he entered the Student Union food court, he ordered his food and went back to his dorm.

Friday night came with an air of happiness encompassing Calvin's dorm room. Alex and Calvin were looking forward to getting away from campus and having a good time. They were going to the student's hang out called Franks. Since they would possibly be drinking, Calvin had arranged for a car to pick them up. Calvin called to make sure Susan was ready. Susan answered the phone in a rushed voice, "Give me ten more minutes, and I will meet you in front of my dorm." Calvin used the additional time to check himself out in the mirror. Alex laughed and said, "Get out of that mirror, Calvin, you look fine. Let's go." With smiles on their faces, Alex and Calvin left to pick up Susan.

In the car, Alex and Susan's conversation was polite but remained cool toward each other. Calvin hoped their attitudes would change as the night progressed. It was crowded in Franks. They didn't want to wait for a table, so they sat at the bar. At the bar, they saw some people they knew from the university. Everyone was talking to the people they knew. They also started looking at the game on one of several television screens throughout the building. The atmosphere reminded Calvin of his high school graduation celebration. This time he felt more comfortable. Calvin was laughing, talking, and even walked to the end of the bar to speak to some classmates he knew.

Everyone was enjoying themselves when Calvin noticed the time. It was late. Calvin knew he had to pack his bags because his parents would be picking him up by noon the next day. He asked Susan and Alex if they were ready to leave. Both of them nodded their heads, yes. Calvin called for a car to pick them up. They were still waiting to settle the bill when the car arrived. Calvin told them he would go out to meet the vehicle. He gave Alex his share of the tab and left.

The darkness of the night made it hard for Calvin to find the car. His eyes glanced across the street and saw a familiar figure. A guy that looked exactly like him wearing the same clothing. It was his doppelgänger. The doppelgänger was standing by the light post displaying that same shy smile and his arms folded. When he saw Calvin looking at him, the doppelgänger waved. "Hey," Calvin shouted, running toward him. The doppelgänger started walking. Calvin started running across the street. He stayed focused on the doppelgänger totally ignoring the oncoming traffic. "Wait," Calvin shouted, reaching for his rosary. At that moment, a car was coming down the street. Calvin was not looking and ran right in front of the car. The driver tried to stop but could not. The vehicle struck Calvin so hard he bounced in the air and hit the ground very hard.

Susan and Alex witnessed the accident, and they started screaming Calvin's name just before the car hit him. They ran to his side. Susan held his hand as Alex called for an ambulance. "Hold on, buddy, the ambulance will be here in a minute," Alex pleaded. In a low voice, Calvin whispered, “Doppelgänger." Susan and Alex responded, "Where, where?". They looked around but didn’t see the doppelgänger. The ambulance arrived and took Calvin to the hospital. Susan and Alex followed them to the hospital in the car they had arranged. They rode to the hospital quietly. When the car pulled into the hospital parking lot, Alex noticed how vivid the sky's colors were. Alex said, "Susan see the sky. It is unusually colorful tonight." "Yes, it is quite beautiful," Susan said in a nervous tone. Susan and Alex looked up to the sky, closed their eyes for a second, and then got out of the car.

Chapter 14

The nurse informed Susan and Alex that Calvin had to have emergency surgery. They were horrified by the unfolding of events. Susan called Calvin's parents and informed them of the accident, Calvin's status, and the hospital's name. Herman and Darlene were already on their way to the campus. His parents told Susan they would be there by noon. Susan and Alex decided to stay in the hospital until Calvin was out of surgery. They fell asleep in the emergency room.

The rising of the sun coming through the windows in the emergency room woke them up. The nurse at the desk informed them Calvin was still in surgery. They dozed back to sleep. Several hours had passed when a doctor came into the emergency room to give them an update on their friend's condition. In the middle of the conversation, Susan saw Calvin's parents come into the hospital. Susan greeted them and introduced his parents to Alex and the doctor. The doctor described Calvin's condition very thoroughly. He emphasized that Calvin was in critical condition. He had been placed in the intensive care unit for observation. The doctor suggested for them to relax in the intensive care waiting room until Calvin woke up. Susan said, "Alex, I am going to stay until Calvin wakes up." "Me too," Alex said in a sad voice. They went to the hospital cafeteria to eat before going to the waiting room.

The waiting room was easy to find. It was located by the elevator enclosed in glass. When the two walked off the elevator, Susan saw Calvin's parents in the waiting room. Susan and Alex asked Calvin's parents had they heard anything about his condition. Herman said no, and Darlene ignored them. It was apparent Darlene was upset. They settled into a chair and waited.

Within the hour, Professor Taylor entered the waiting room. Susan had called him earlier that morning and told him about the accident. Susan introduced him to Calvin's parents. Professor Taylor reached out to shake Darlene's hand.

Instead of shaking his hand, Darlene started ranting about the accident happening because of the Professor, Susan, and Alex. Herman tried to calm her down, but she would not stop. Darlene accused Susan and Alex of playing mind games with Calvin. She accused Professor Taylor of illegally putting Calvin in a cryosleep state. All of them started pointing fingers accusing each other. The conversation got heated, then, all of a sudden, Susan looked toward the elevator and froze. Everyone stopped talking and stared at Susan. Susan acted as if she'd seen a ghost. She raised her hand and pointed at a guy entering the elevator. The guy looked just like Calvin, same pants and shirt. "Calvin, Calvin!" they shouted. Alex said in a low voice, "That's not Calvin; it's his doppelgänger." Herman said, "What is going on?" About that time the elevator's door closed. Everyone ran out of the room to the nurse's station to find Calvin's room, except for Professor Taylor. The Professor ran down the stairs trying to catch the elevator, saying, "I am going to get to the bottom of this." The person at the nursing station told them Calvin's room number. She tried to tell them they could not go into the room, but they went anyway.

They entered the room. Calvin was lying in bed hooked to several tubes. The tubes were attached to a monitor. Susan shouted his name because she was shocked to see him there. Hearing his name, Calvin gradually opened his eyes. "Susan," he whispered. Calvin was saying something in a low exhausted tone. Susan had to bend down and put her ear down close to his mouth to hear what he was saying. "I am here, Calvin," Susan replied with a sad voice. Calvin proceeded to tell her, "I was dreaming, I was flying above the clouds." What did he say, they asked? She raised her finger, giving a signal to wait a minute. Calvin continued, "When I woke up standing at the foot of the bed was my doppelgänger." "What?" she asked. Taking a deep breath, Calvin said, "Yes, he was standing at the foot of my bed." Susan was so confused, but she wanted to project a sense of calmness; she told him, "It will be alright, Calvin." Calvin could barely speak but said, "No, you don't understand he said, never to land. Then the doppelgänger turned around and left." Calvin stopped talking and closed his eyes.

"What did he say?" They asked. Professor Taylor entered the room and said, "I could not catch him." Susan told them what Calvin said. Alex looked shocked and commented, "Oh no, he said never to land, that's the omen." "What omen?" Darlene asked. "Death" Alex said with tears in his eyes. "Nonsense! I don't believe that" Herman said with an angry voice. Just then Calvin mumbled, "Never to land." His eyes were still closed. They looked at each other in shock.

Then the monitor's alarm went off. It made a continuous loud beeping sound. The nurse rushed in and started checking Calvin's vital signs. Within a couple of seconds the beeping stopped and a flat line displayed on the monitor. The nurse glance at the monitor. She dropped her hands to her side and with a sad look on her face said, "I am sorry, he's gone."

www.ingramcontent.com/pod-product-compliance
Lightning Source LLC
LaVergne TN
LVHW050958080826
845145LV00009B/2351

* 9 7 8 1 7 3 3 3 5 9 5 0 4 *